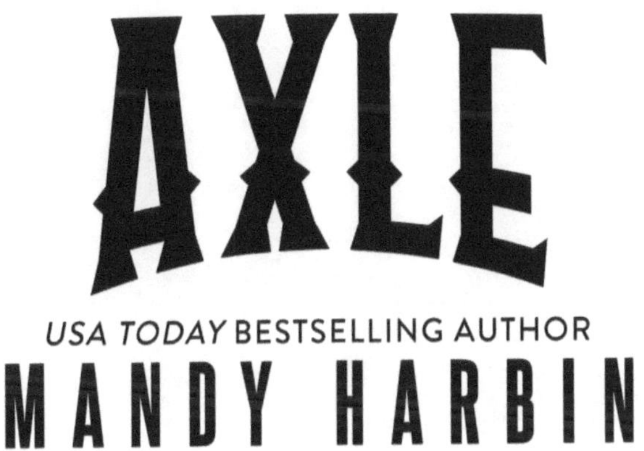

USA TODAY BESTSELLING AUTHOR

MANDY HARBIN

Caitlin Cooper sat nervously as she gazed over the crowd. There were more people here than she'd anticipated, though a Bronze Star Ceremony was sure to be the talk of the town and draw even those normally uninterested in current affairs out of the woodwork. An event such as this garnered national attention, so in addition to the community and local politicians, there were also members of congress and congressional committees in attendance. It was odd to see such a mixed crowd and recognize so many of the people—both personally and professionally—especially when she hadn't been back in years. Not that she'd planned it that way, but as a news correspondent covering the War on Terror, her assignments rarely kept her on U.S. soil, much less in her old stomping grounds.

Of course, she had cut her journalism teeth covering local news in Arkansas when she'd been fresh out of college. She'd covered all kinds of stories from festivals to police beat stuff to eventually local politics. The turning point in her career had been when she'd interviewed the former governor regarding his stance on capital punishment when a bill to repeal the death penalty had failed to get the support it needed to pass. Though the story itself hadn't been the defining moment. In fact, it had nothing to do with it. She shivered at the memory and chaffed her arms as she thought back to the night when she'd reported live from the governor's mansion, and the cameraman had left to load some of his gear. She'd been alone with the governor's then-aide—and the current lieutenant governor—when he made an unwelcome pass at her. He hadn't crossed any official lines, but he hadn't reacted pleasantly to her rejection.

Relief had flooded her when her colleague returned for the last case, and she'd quickly fallen into step beside him as he exited the building. She learned that night how important it was to get to know her cameraman because he—or she—could become a necessary lifeline in this business. But more importantly, the encounter that night had oddly given her the kick in the pants to leave the comfort of her home state and reach for her dreams. She figured if she was going to get hit on in her own backyard by questionable politicians, there was no reason to fear the news outside of Arkansas.

If she was ballsy, she would go over to the scumbag politician now and thank him. Of course, he wouldn't be able to see it for the sarcasm it was.

WWCAD? That had been her internal mantra whenever she felt at a crossroads. *What would Christiane Amanpour do?* The woman inspired her. She was the reason Caitlin wanted to go into journalism. Within a month of leaving home, Caitlin had landed the job of a lifetime as a correspondent with a major twenty-four-hour news station in Atlanta. She'd paid her dues covering stories on the war, even had been sent on location to the Middle East multiple times, though not right in the action. Always on the outskirts of any real danger, tucked neatly within the press corp.

When Caitlin's gaze landed on a group of tough-looking men entering the room, she quickly dropped it to her notebook as heat tinged the tips of her ears.

One of those guys was Hunter Anderson. There had been a time in her life whenever he walked into a room she'd swear her heart was going to jump right out of her chest. She'd had it bad for him growing up and should laugh now over her awkward adolescence and silly crush. If only she could tell her fourteen-year-old self that one day Hunter would be in the same room as her and he *not* be the one making her heart pound like crazy. She was certain if she could actually go back in time and tell herself this, her *mini-me* would totally ignore her. Caitlin had spent an embarrassing amount of time in her bedroom listening to love songs on her iPod while staring at his picture in the yearbook...and that was when she hadn't gotten to spend the night with her best friend and Hunter's sister, Heather, sleeping under the same roof as him.

Oh how times had changed. She wasn't a little girl pining for a boy. The sight of Hunter did nothing to her anymore. Her racing heart and sweaty palms were because of the man standing next to him.

Axle.

Axle Landry. She knew there was no avoiding him today. Hell, he was the reason she was even here. Her starving gaze wouldn't be denied either, breaking her mental command not to stare at the man who'd stolen her heart in the desert. God, he still looked perfect, even though he walked with a cane now. His arms rippled as he leaned slightly into it as he moved. She remembered just how strong he was when he lifted her in the heat of passion just a few months ago, and she'd bet her life his battle injury wouldn't slow him down for a second. She had firsthand knowledge just how determined that man could be when he set his sights on something he wanted.

Several people in the crowd near him came over, shook his hand, and clapped him on the back, probably thanking him for his service to our country. She forced herself to look away, to look back down at her notepad. *Where's my pen?* Oh, the irony. She glanced around the floor beside her to check if it had fallen once she'd been seated. It wasn't there, and she huffed as she grabbed her bag to dig for a new one. She'd bought a new box of them when she'd gotten back to the States and had made a point to shove several in all of her cases and in her car, determined to never need to borrow another pen again. Instinctively, she looked up, knowing her hand would land on one without much effort.

As if he was her beacon, she looked to Axle. And froze.

He stared right at her.

Caitlin swallowed, locked in his hot gaze, instantly taken back to *other* times he'd looked at her just as intensely but for a completely different reason. She couldn't look away now even if she wanted to, and she didn't. She'd missed him so much since the last day she saw him...the day everything went to shit, and they'd been ripped apart by circumstance.

He took a step, then another, slowly making his way to the stage without breaking eye contact just yet. She wanted to run to him and help him walk, but she knew beyond any doubt he'd hate her even more if she offered him any assistance. He was a strong man.

He was a proud man.

And now, he was a disabled man. A former SEAL

injured in the prime of his life. The career he carefully nurtured for so many years completely obliterated.

All because of her.

She should look away, make this easier on him, but she couldn't. Not yet. Because she knew once this ceremony was over, that would be it. Any silly hope she'd clung to would be gone. She'd be back in Atlanta, and he'd be here, getting used to his new, unwanted life.

After today, she would never see Axle Landry again.

CHAPTER ONE

Three months ago.

"You wanted to see me, sir?" Caitlin Cooper asked after knocking on her supervisor's doorjamb. Jack Roper's door stayed open when he was in the office, and if it wasn't for him wearing a different set of clothes each day, Caitlin would wonder if the man actually ever went home. Not a week went by without him uttering the phrase, "*the news never sleeps.*" She figured he applied that rule to himself as much as possible.

"Come in, Cooper." Jack didn't look up from the pile of papers on his desk. The man had four computer monitors spread out behind him, but he came from the era when pen and paper were the gold standard, even though their media was television and not written periodicals.

She took a seat opposite him and placed her hands in her lap. She'd been on her way back from lunch when she'd gotten his message to see him immediately. There'd been no time to swing by her desk to retrieve her tablet to take any possible notes. Unlike her boss, Caitlin enjoyed the use of modern technology.

"You know, hours ago, the US conducted an air strike utilizing the largest non-nuclear weapon in its arsenal."

Caitlin nodded. "They're calling it the mother of all bombs."

"It's a MOAB, Massive Ordnance Air Blast, but yeah." He picked up a piece of paper and handed it to her. She took it and glanced down at the official press release regarding the strike.

"Word is they took out ISIS tunnels and bunkers."

"You think there's more they're not saying."

Jack leveled his stare at her. "There's always more that they're not saying. Remember the Khataba raid? US special missions operators killed five civilians, including two pregnant women. NATO and the UN claimed to know nothing about it. Journalists dug in and discovered US JSOC operators were involved and removed the bullets from the bodies in an effort to cover up the mistake."

She remembered when the story broke. The local journalist had been detained. The military did not want the truth to get out and had spun some story about how the women had already been killed by insurgents sometime prior to the special ops arrival. Once the truth came out, the whole incident had led to an even bigger story. The unprecedented power of the JSOC—Joint Special Operators Command—shedding light on their drone and snatch, grab, assassinate programs. Caitlin could appreciate the complications of war. It was messy and gritty. She, like many other Americans, owed a debt of gratitude to the men and women fighting for their freedom and prayed for their safe return home. She understood there were covert units throughout all branches of the military and federal agencies. But this one? It was the only one that reported directly to the White House, making it a paramilitary arm of whatever administration was in office. An organization that handled the most sensitive counter-terrorism attacks all over the *world*, not just in active war zones. The revelation was shocking, and she figured more would come to light about the unit's questionable authority. But, a year later, JSOC's efforts led to the death of Osama Bin Laden, the most hated man in the world and founder of the al-Qaeda terrorist organization, effectively silencing critics and burying further stories.

"I remember."

Jack sat back in his chair, staring at her. She wanted to squirm at his perusal, but she didn't. She had a feeling he was assessing her for a reason. No way did she want to show any kind of weakness.

"I need someone on the ground at Nangarhar. Initial reports are thirty-six casualties consisting of ISIS militants. Reconnaissance units are going in, so that number is sure to go up. I sent Harris last week to cover the bombing in Syria. The administration is facing heat with that decision since more reports are coming through that the US may have bombed a mosque. No way can I pull Harris off that assignment and send him to Afghanistan to cover the MOAB strike, which may have been better planned and not reveal any casualty cover-ups."

"You're sending me." It wasn't a question. There was a reason he'd wanted to see her immediately rather than wait and discuss this tomorrow at the team's daily status meetings when new assignments were discussed and assigned.

"This will be your first assignment reporting outside the wire."

She nodded. She'd covered several stories in the Middle East over the last couple of years. It was still dangerous, but there'd been a certain amount of comfort reporting from inside the wired walls and heavily armed boundaries of the coalition base. A surge of nervous energy engulfed her, but she worked hard to regulate her breathing to keep her boss from noticing anything other than sheer determination to get the job done.

"You fly out tonight and rendezvous with the cameraman currently on rotation, filming general footage of the war. If you find anything worth noting, you'll film your story and submit your clip for airing. If it's a hot story, you'll get live coverage. Any questions?"

She was reeling but totally ready. If she got the scoop on any military cover-up, it could propel her career. "No, sir."

"Good. Report to me once you arrive. Since you don't have your notebook, I'll email you the names of some of our contacts that'll get you headed in the right direction."

Crap. She didn't need him to think she walked around unprepared. "Just came back from lunch, sir. I'll have my tablet on the ready."

"And your notebook. Never forget. The pen is mightier than the sword."

She seriously didn't think the adage applied to war zones, but no way was she voicing that.

He rose from his desk, extending his hand. She shook it. "Good luck."

"Thank you, sir. Any advice?"

"The details could be anywhere. Leave no stone unturned. Think like a source and become the story."

"Thanks. I won't let you down."

Caitlin high-tailed it out of his office, digging for her phone as she made her way to her desk. She pulled up her contacts and called Heather Anderson, one of her oldest friends.

"Hey, girl. Can't wait to see you this weekend," Heather said as way of answering the call.

A twinge of regret stabbed at Caitlin. She hadn't been home to Arkansas in years and hadn't made an effort to see Heather since she'd moved back. She and Heather got together from time-to-time when a favorite band was playing in a major city or one of their mutual friends organized weekend getaways in Chicago or Vegas. When Heather was attending college in Dallas, Caitlin flew out there a few times to meet up. Although life had taken her in another direction, she loved it when she got to see Heather, so she hated she was going to have to cancel this visit. "About that," she started slowly.

"Oh no. I know that tone. And here I was just thinking if I can get away from my over protective brother for like two seconds, I'd give you the low-down on all the naughty girls' night out stuff I'd planned."

She heard a distinctively male voice mutter something, and Caitlin knew Hunter was probably hovering a little too close to Heather. There was a time that Caitlin would have dropped anything for a chance to be in the same room as him. But time changed things. He'd moved off, which had given the time for her little heart to focus on other boys. Not that Caitlin had time to date now, but even if she did and was still interested in Hunter, that man was head over heels for Heather's current BFF, Maya Carmichael. Ironic, he ended up falling for a friend of Heather's, and Caitlin wasn't it. Oh well, it was never meant to be. She never thought much about her insane crush these days, but she felt a heat creep up her throat at the sound of his voice. That heat had nothing to do with attraction and everything to do with the embarrassment of her younger years.

"Caitlin?"

"Huh?" she asked, realizing she'd zoned out for a few seconds and hadn't heard what Heather had said.

"I said, what's the story about? Because I know you ditching plans has to be because of work."

She was at her desk now and started shoving things into her laptop case. "Sorry, yeah. I'm investigating the bomb that was just dropped in Afghanistan."

"Are you going to the bomb site?"

"Yeah. The mother of all bombs is a story in and of itself, but there could be more." She didn't elaborate any. At this point, it was just speculation, and she had an ethical code not to spread misleading information.

"But isn't that dangerous? I mean, I know Afghanistan is dangerous anyway, but you're going out to where they just dropped a bomb. It's an active combat zone."

"Yeah, it's dangerous, but I can't focus on that. I have to fly out tonight."

"Tonight?" she squeaked. "Jeez. This is happening too fast! You need time to prepare before you go trotting off into a war zone—"

"Caitlin." But the voice coming through the phone now was no longer Heather's. It was deep and authoritative. Her heartbeat stuttered and then kicked up. She figured it was because Hunter startled her when he'd snapped her name.

"Give me back my phone," she heard Heather protest in the distance.

"What's your ETA in Afghanistan?" he asked her, ignoring his sister's continued pleas in the background.

"I-I don't know. I fly out tonight. I imagine sometime tomorrow night, why?"

"Who's your contact?"

"Um, I don't know. I literally found out I'm leaving like thirty seconds ago. The information is being emailed to me as we speak. I'm loading up my computer now and then heading to my apartment to pack."

"Forward it to me before you leave your office."

She paused, wondering where this stern attitude was coming from. "Why?" she asked, drawing the word out.

"All the color drained out of Heather's face when you told her where you were going, so she's freaking out. And for good reason."

"I know she's worried, but that still doesn't tell me why you want to know."

He huffed, his frustration clearly coming through the cell signal. "Because, believe it or not, I do know some people."

"In the military?" she asked, thinking she would've heard if he'd joined when he moved away. Since it was all quiet, she assumed he was doing something shady and didn't want to risk figuring it out. Ignorance was only bliss to reporters when it came to people they were close to. Besides, even if he had joined, he was back in Arkansas now, working at a garage.

"I'm not at liberty to say."

"Mmm-hmm." She rolled her eyes and was sure the sarcasm in her voice was apparent. "You're a mechanic, not a solider."

"You're a reporter, not a solider."

"Hunter—"

"You're heading right into the line of fire. Heather's worried, and you're like a sister to me. I want to make sure you're safe."

You're like a sister to me.

At least he'd never come out and said those words when she was ogling him from across the room. They would have crushed her little infatuated heart. Now, she felt a different kind of warmth. He was worried for her safety and that deflated any argument she'd been building in her head.

"Okay, all right. I'll send you the info. I'll even check in with Heather after I get there. Happy?"

"And your parents."

She sighed. Jeez, if her friend's *brother* was acting this worried, she could only imagine how her dad was going to take this news. She'd already planned on calling them next. "Got it, Hunter."

There would be no arguing with him. She might have been crushing on him as a boy and jumped to do whatever he said, but now he was a hard man commanding authority and expecting compliance. It was obvious he'd been through some major stuff in his life and had changed over the years. She thought of him working at the garage during the time Colonel Shepard was there and the shit hit the fan. She'd been relieved she was out of the country on assignment, so she hadn't been tasked with getting to the bottom of it. Heather had been away at college and not around when it happened—and seemingly swept under the rug. Her friend had been spared the fallout. More than once, though, Caitlin had wondered how it affected Hunter.

He must've handed the phone back to Heather because it was her voice that came through next. "Please, be careful. Find some strong solider with guns hanging off every limb to protect you."

Caitlin wanted to chuckle at the image of that, but the muffled words of Hunter stopped her. "I'm already on it."

"What does that mean?" she yelled, hoping he could hear her.

"It means, he's right," Heather said. "He has connections."

"How does a mechanic get military connections?"

"Umm... There's a lot you don't know. Maybe it's time you were told."

This sounded like a major conversation, and she was already running late. "When I get back from this assignment, you can tell me over a bottle of wine."

Heather chuckled. "You might want something stronger than that."

"Please tell me it's because I'd have just been in a war zone." It wasn't a question because she already knew the answer. This discussion would have nothing to do with Afghanistan.

"Call me when you get there," was all she said and hung up.

———

AXLE LANDRY MADE his way to see the Major General but had no clue as to the reason he'd been called in. He should be out training with his team and getting ready to head to the Gulf for exercises. When he'd asked his CO why he'd been singled out when he wasn't even the team leader of his unit, Axle had gotten his ass chewed about following orders. Hell, he knew the drill. He'd been in the military for years, having re-upped again a few years ago. It was all he knew. Mostly.

There'd been a time early on when he thought he was going to switch to the private sector. He'd been on block leave working with the Orion team in cooperation with other military units at the time, but once their targets were neutralized, the group had been dismantled. He figured it could have taken on more operations on rotation once all the bugs typical with any pilot program were worked out, but after Oz had fallen in love with Bryn while on that assignment, his former team leader retired from military life to be with her. She'd been on the run from the mafia and Oz had been super protective of her. He had no idea where they moved off to. Zeke, on the other hand, had gone back to the bureau, and Axle remembered thinking Zeke's decision probably had a little to do with being near Katie, the federal agent who'd worked on that assignment with them. Anybody with functioning eyeballs saw the man had a thing for her.

The three original Orion team members' lives had all taken different paths, and Axle had been no different in carving out his future. He was now part of DEVGRU, more commonly known as SEAL Team Six. After bin Laden had been KIA, he knew the media wouldn't stop until the group assigned to take him out had been identified. Those guys had been from Red Squadron. Axle was in the Black Squadron, but he knew those guys. Like many groups within the military, there was a camaraderie among the naval special warfare group.

Axle had worked hard to get where he was and was damn good at his job. He was one of the best snipers in the military, but he'd be lying if he said the decision to retire didn't weigh on him. The war on terror ended up being a much larger campaign than anyone thought back when it had started. With the war in Iraq and Afghanistan and against ISIS, the US needed all the servicemen they could get. It made him feel a little guilty when he thought about not reenlisting again.

He was proud of his service, but being in the military meant he wasn't around to help his dad with the car shop back home. His father had recently retired and closed the business he grew up helping with. If Axle completed his military career, he could always open it back up and continue the legacy his father started. Some of the best years of his life were spent under the hood of a car.

His contract would be up later this year, assuming they didn't involuntarily extend it another twelve months. That, too, was a definite possibility, and nothing he could do about it if it happened. Any decision on what he could do after leaving the military would have to wait until he actually knew he could be discharged. No use in thinking about that now. A lot could happen before then.

It was oh-eight on the dot when he reached the door and rapped on it.

"Come in."

Axle entered and saluted. "Commander Axle Landry reporting, sir."

"At ease."

Axle dropped his hand and stood in proper position, awaiting further command.

"You're aware we had a C-130 drop a gift in Nangarhar."

He was more than aware. Axle was pretty sure it was still the talk of the base. "Yes, sir."

Major General Ethan Burge regarded him for several seconds. "Have a seat, Commander," he finally said. Axle took the chair directly across from the man who was one of the hardest ever created in the US military. He was the deputy commander of operations and intelligence of CJTF-OIR. The Combined Joint Task Force was only a couple of years old and headquartered in Kuwait, so Axle had never had a chance to meet him personally. When CJTF was implemented, he'd remembered his days with Orion and had been hopeful it would be successful where his own endeavor had not. Besides having similar experiences of working with a joint task force, Major General Burge was also a fellow SEAL, so there was the unspoken brotherhood bond as well. The big difference between them was that this man before him was powerful. He worked under the US Lieutenant General Stanley Tanner, the leader at the helm of CJTF on Operation Inherent Resolve, which had been established to degrade and destroy ISIS.

"My CO didn't provide any intel as to the nature of this meeting." Then he quickly added, "Although, I'm always ready and available to serve without question."

Burge raised an eyebrow. "Your CO hasn't been cleared to receive the details. He was none too happy being stonewalled."

That explained the hostility when Axle had tried to ask for clarification. No one liked being out of the loop, especially when the loop involved his subordinate men, but this information only raised more questions.

"You're a sniper."

"Yes, sir."

"Your records indicate you're the best. Not only with confirmed kills, but with accuracy."

If he'd been curious about this meeting earlier, he was downright confused now. For some reason, the Major General had dug into his evaluations. Carefully wording his reply, he said, "I don't keep up with individual statistics, sir. I'm part of a team."

"Good answer."

"It's the truth." He'd said it as if that was all the explanation the Major General needed, but the other man just stared. The silence was thick and almost painful. Axle tried to think of why his shooting skills were important if his entire team hadn't been part of his meeting. Immediately, he mentally ran through months and months of operations, wondering if he'd done something that would require reprimanding him. The thought was sickening, but he came up blank, unable to think of any reason his performance would have him in this room with the Major General.

"You're also up for reenlistment."

Axle blinked, but masked any other reaction. "Yes, sir."

"Hmm...I see."

Shit. "I don't make those decisions until it's time, sir," he quickly added. It was the truth. Sort of.

"Fair enough." Burge nodded slowly. "I've also learned you have a better than average understanding of vehicles."

These questions seemed to be all over the place, but Axle was smart enough to know there was a point to all of this. "Yes, sir. My father owned a garage in Georgia. He's retired now."

Burge shifted in his seat, leaning slightly closer. "I'm putting you on a special op, Commander." Axle stood a little taller with this news. "There's a favor I owe a former teammate of mine. A Ms. Caitlin Cooper is in transit to our desert digs, and she's going to need protection. That's where you come in."

Protection? "Is there a price on her head?" he asked seriously as he scanned his thoughts on the name. It was familiar to him, but he couldn't place who she was. It wasn't uncommon for famous people to come and show their support for troops through various shows and speeches. With name recognition came added threats, so they heightened security whenever someone scheduled a visit.

"There's a price on everyone's head. She, in particular, is a journalist coming to cover the MOAB strike."

Jesus, he hoped like hell he hadn't groaned at the word

journalist. Unlike those who briefly stopped in to entertain them, reporters were a different beast. He understood the freedom of the press and all that business, but this was war. Her face still didn't flash in his head with the new information, but he'd seen many correspondents embedded over the years on his tours and they were always where the action was. Being on a SEAL team, and a sniper at that, meant he'd never had to deal with them personally.

Until now.

"Originally from Arkansas, she's lived in Georgia for years now." Burge frowned briefly before continuing in a no-nonsense manner. "You're experienced with automotive technology, so if a transport gets hit, you can mitigate the damage and get her to safety. You're shooting record is exemplary, so you can take out threats from afar, and you're a SEAL, so I know you're skilled in lethal hand-to-hand combat. You're familiar with the Achin District since your team had been tasked with scoping it out prior to the order to strike, and she'll no doubt request passage. Your team isn't currently on assignment, so pulling you away for a few weeks to work with her won't cause any disruption to our primary mission here. You even have the state of Georgia in common."

The bricks were falling into place now and landing one-by-one on his head. His superior hadn't meant *protection* as in taking out identified threats against her. "This is a babysitting job," he said without thinking.

"More like you'll be her personal bodyguard. You'll be given a small crew to assist in her protection and to fight combatants, but she's your primary objective. You're all over her like morning dew. She won't be able to burp without you identifying what she had for lunch. Am I clear?"

"Yes, sir," he said, but the words felt like they'd been

muttered on autopilot as anger settled in. He stared straight ahead, wondering who in the world he pissed off to land this kind of karma.

"Sorry, sailor. I know it seems you drew the short straw on this, and well, because of circumstances, you did. It might've been born out of personal reasons, but make no mistake, this isn't some unsanctioned op. Lt. General Stanley Tanner signed off on this. He did so because I asked him to, which means not only will you be reporting directly to me, but he's fully aware of this assignment and will be kept abreast of all the details surrounding it."

Holy shit. It shocked the hell out of him that he'd be reporting directly to the Major General, but to hear the Lt. General would be keeping tabs on him too? Axle had never had this close of a direct line to the more political officers. This was a crap assignment, no ifs, ands, or buts about it. But it'd be a highly visible one. He would have to make sure he followed protocol without any errors. Good thing he was a stickler for obeying the rules anyway. This time, however, important people would be watching him. Not a team, *him.* If he screwed up, it'd be his ass, but if he showed them how diligent and methodical he could be then maybe..."

"You do this assignment without fail, you'll be going places, Landry. Fast," Burge said aloud what Axle's thought refused to finish in silence. "Assuming you decide to reenlist that is," he added with a smirk.

Could a babysitting job really propel his military career more so than actual battles he'd fought? *It's not what you know...it's who you know.* Yeah, it was entirely possible. Having a personal connection to the people in charge couldn't hurt.

Unless he screwed this up somehow.

No way was Axle going to let that happen.

"To be clear, you are protection. Period. Not a source. I don't want your name anywhere in her reports. You are not cleared to answer questions about the mission in the Achin District prior to the strike. The fact that you've recently been to the area was a determining factor in approving you for this role, but that doesn't mean the military is giving her free access to sensitive intel. Understood?"

"Sir, yes, sir," he said with more conviction than before.

Keep my eyes open and mouth shut. He had a job to do, not that he had a choice. Axle had to take the assignment whether he liked it or not, but at least there could be something in it for him in the end. He had no problem keeping his personal knowledge of that prior mission to himself. Secrecy was par for the course in special operations anyway.

He had a lot of questions running through his head, but he wouldn't waste the Major General's time. As soon as he got back, he'd power up his CO's laptop and get those answers, starting with the most important question running loose in his mind.

Just who was Caitlin Cooper, and why was this journalist so important that the Lieutenant General was uprooting not only him, but a team of men he'd oversee all for the purpose of guarding her?

CHAPTER TWO

Caitlin was exhausted. Tired to her bones from her trip to Afghanistan, and she'd only just gotten here. Upon landing, she'd had to go through what she likened to the military's version of customs to get access to the base, and that hadn't included actual customs along the way. She needed a shower followed by a five-hour nap and a five-pound cheeseburger.

WWCAD? She doubted her professional idol would stuff her face and whine about needing some grub and a tub. Caitlin shook the thoughts of creature comforts away. If she was lucky, she'd only be here a couple of weeks. Troop deployments were a heck of a lot longer than any short trip she would experience. She'd do well to remember that and not complain, even internally. She knew this. She blamed being tired for the lapse, but she needed to ignore her fatigue and focus on her job. If she fixated on every yawn her body produced, that was another moment she wasn't thinking about her work.

Or her safety.

Her dad had served in Desert Storm and hadn't taken

the news of her current assignment lightly. She could still hear the warnings he'd given her echoing in her ears. *"Follow orders... You will not risk your life for the story... Don't let some randy soldier into your panties..."* That last one had almost made her laugh. Almost. Her dad was normally a big ol' softy who loved to joke, having long ago left the military behind for a boring desk job and life in suburbia. His haunted eyes shone brightly on the rare occasions he talked of his tours. The added veil of the video call yesterday did nothing to hide the permanent despair long buried in them. But he was her dad. He'd be concerned if she was going on vacation alone to Florida.

As she'd promised, she sent texts to her parents and Heather, letting them know she'd gotten there safely. She'd call later when she wasn't about to pass out and when the time change wasn't working against them.

"Ms. Cooper?" a tall, dark-haired man asked. He sported several days' growth on his chin. "I'm Lorenzo Ricci, the videographer working with you on this assignment."

She hopped as she hefted her carry-on more securely to her shoulder and stuck out her hand. "Nice to meet you, Mr. Ricci."

"Lorenzo, please."

"Caitlin," she said in way of agreement before dropping her hand. "What can you tell me about the bombing?"

"All in due time, *Caitlin*," a man said walking up from behind Lorenzo. She looked over at him, irritation pricking at how he'd said her name, but before she formed a response, she noticed he wasn't the only man in uniform close by. There were several men standing with their legs slightly apart and their hands behind their backs all staring directly at her. Her gaze slid to each one before she looked up at the man who'd spoken to her seconds ago and invaded her personal space now. "You have to be briefed on procedure and sign some documentation before you're allowed access to any information. Follow me." He turned as if not needing a response from her.

She wasn't surprised there was more formality involved. Although she'd never reported on the front lines, this wasn't her first assignment in the midst of a war. Tired or not, his tone rankled her. The least they could do was not schedule this introduction before she had a chance to check in at her hotel and drop off her bags.

And eat.

And sleep. Definitely that.

She knew she should fall into step behind him without question, but before she could command her feet to move, her mouth opened. "Who are you?" she almost snapped.

The brute in combat boots had only taken one step when her voice filled the air between them. He froze, and it seemed as if the men standing in a half circle around her got stiller.

The man's hands flexed as if he was going to fist them but then thought better of it before turning to face her once again. "Commander Axle Landry. The man tasked with keeping your backside protected." He hesitated and then added, "Ma'am."

"Nice to meet you, *Axle*." She wasn't sure if she mastered the same tone he'd taken with her name, but she gave it her best shot. Somewhere in the back of her mind was a warning not to anger the big, scary—and if she was completely honest, *hot*—guy. But it wasn't as if this man was her superior, nor did she need to butter him up to get him to talk. She had a list of names of people who'd been in the area before and after the bombing and had committed those to memory. There was no Axle Landry on her list. She was too tired for this.

One of the men coughed, sounding as if covering a laugh.

Without hesitation, Axle stomped right up to him and yelled in his face. Caitlin didn't catch everything he said. Something about what the man found so funny with some colorful words tossed in, but it was enough to jerk the sleep from her eyes. The military dynamic fascinated her, but the yelling and posturing was something she never felt comfortable with. She understood the need to keep members in line, but sometimes it felt as if it was really overkill. Like right now. But she wasn't here to question the inner workings of the military itself.

The younger-looking guy paled a little, but barked his responses, keeping in time with Axle's forceful questions.

The rest of his introduction finally slammed into her. *The man tasked with keeping your backside protected.*

She gritted her teeth to keep from barking out Hunter's name as frustrated realization dawned. *This* extra muscle had to be his doing. She got the horrible suspicion this man would also do his best to make sure she didn't go snooping around any restricted areas while on base. All under the guise of protection.

When Axle finished ripping the guy a new one, he stomped back to her, so she had to push away thoughts of Hunter's meddling for now. "Let's get something straight, Caitlin. I'm not happy about this assignment. I should be with my SEAL team running exercises in preparation for our next rotation, not watching every waking move you make. I wasn't trained to be someone's snarling twenty-four-seven guard dog."

"Guard dog?" she asked incredulously as she crossed her arms. "At least they enjoy their service."

"Don't act irritated with me." He waved away her rebuttal.

Ha! Who was acting?

"I'm the one who's position got sidelined for your career. I'd much rather be hiding in the dark, taking out marks with lethal precision, but the powers-that-be want me to babysit a journalist instead. If anyone has a right to be irritated, it's me."

"Why don't you tell me how you really feel?" she asked with heavy sarcasm.

He continued as if she hadn't spoken. "Someone above my paygrade believes you have a target on your back, and they hope I can take 'em out before they take you down. Doesn't mean my service comes with patience or a smile. Saving your life will have to be *service* enough."

Target on my back? She blinked at him. His words were harsh, but the mental image he just painted was more powerful than anything he'd spewed. Jack hadn't said anything to her about someone targeting her. Was this a standard concern for media personnel when reporting outside the wire? Surely, she'd have heard that before, if not when reporting on wars herself inside the safer areas then from her fellow journalists when talking shop.

Had Hunter somehow known this? She didn't see how, but maybe? There was a lot she didn't know about him. She wasn't sure what to think of all this, and the reality that there was a lot she wasn't aware of slowly came crashing over her. She shook a little and sucked in a deep breath. This was the first time since learning of the mission that she felt real fear. She'd been nervous, sure, anxious even, and most recently, exhausted. But not fearful. Why had it settled in now? It felt silly that it took a hulking man being assigned to her to pull away whatever wool she'd had over her eyes. Not her boss, or Hunter, or even her dad had accomplished that.

Part of her want to reply something snappy back at him, but that side of her was hiding behind the other part whose knees threatened to buckle under the weight of this new feeling coursing through her. There was so much she had to suss out that didn't even pertain to the story itself. When she found her voice, she simply said, "I understand."

She didn't, though. Not really.

He stared, and for the briefest of moments, an emotion crossed his gaze that looked like regret, but it had happened so quickly she couldn't be sure. "Follow me," he said in the same clipped tone from earlier, but without the added ire.

She obeyed, and Lorenzo walked beside her. The other men who'd been standing in front of her waited until she passed before falling into step with them.

Not with them. *Around* them. As if they'd formed some protective barrier, blocking her and the cameraman from view. They were still on base, so the action felt unnecessary, which only spiked this new feeling she was processing.

They walked into a makeshift room built with exposed plywood walls. Contained inside in the center was a folding table surrounded by metal chairs. Nothing else existed in the small area. Axle motioned for her to sit before turning to grab a stack of papers from the end of the table.

"I don't have a PowerPoint to show you the dangers of war in some feeble attempt to express the significance of what could happen if you don't follow orders. You'll just have to listen to the words I have to say."

"I'm good at paying attention," she said without looking at him, ready to get this part over with.

"Good. That just might keep you from having to witness any horrors firsthand." The urge to volley a retort was sudden, but she suppressed it. She knew whatever she was going to say would have been out of more fear and not at all helpful. When she didn't remark, he continued his spiel.

Axle's lecture was long and detailed. He started with the purpose of their overall objective there before moving into what was expected of the men and women both professionally and personally. Throughout his discussion, her fear eased, which she attributed to Axle's matter-of-fact vibe. And *then* he went into the rules of conduct of an embedded journalist, making sure she was clear on her role. Irritation began to bubble again because she was well aware of what her role was, but she ignored her immediate reaction for now. He had a job of keeping her safe, and she told herself he was just making sure she did her part to make his mission easier. "Any questions so far?"

"No."

"You will not at any time carry a weapon. Ever," he said, leveling a stare at her.

"Why?" Not that she'd brought any with her. She didn't own a gun, and it wasn't as if she could carry a knife on the plane. Although she could have put one in her checked luggage. Maybe she should have.

"Because you are a non-combatant. You are not here to engage in battle. This is not my rule. It is policy."

In theory, she understood this. She'd never considered the need of a weapon before because she'd always reported from a military base where there'd been thousands of men sporting guns and rifles, so the very idea of her needing to carry something on her person had never crossed her mind. Her fear from earlier was back, rearing its ugly head. She nodded, worried her voice would betray her renewed fright. If Hunter wanted the fear of Jesus in her, he'd succeeded.

Axle continued, going over the laundry list of conditions working with an active military unit, such as not reporting any intel that could compromise any unit's position, classified weaponry, and details of future missions she might become privy to, just to name a few. She understood the need. She was a civilian working with the military, and at any time she could learn things not meant for public consumption that could put the lives of the men and women serving at risk.

When he finished his speech, he slid contracts across the table to her and Lorenzo.

"Read these and sign." He leveled a no-argument glare at her.

She took the documentation and began thumbing through it, her mind racing as she read over the words in ink that Axle had said aloud over the last hour. It was one thing to be told something in a briefing and a completely different thing to be obligated to agree to it in writing.

Caitlin could appreciate the need for secrecy. She did. But she also knew, at the end of the day, she had a job to do. One the military and department officials might not be pleased with if she uncovered information they preferred stayed hidden. She would have to follow their rules but be ready to defend her stance on reporting the news. She read every line very carefully to make sure there wasn't anything hidden in there that would expressly prohibit her from doing her job. When she felt satisfied she wasn't agreeing to anything she couldn't live with, she reached for her bag.

"What are you doing?" Axle asked.

She looked up, but continued rummaging. "Um, getting a pen."

He yanked one out of his pocket and slid it across the table. She caught it before it could pass her, but instead of using it immediately, she stared at the thing. It was no ordinary pen. It was black metal with ridges and planes and felt much sturdier than any she'd ever used before. She turned it around in her hand, exploring it further, even tossing it up to feel the weight of it as it landed back in her palm.

"It's a tactical pen. Push the plunger." If he'd given her those instructions as if talking to a child, her cheeks would've flamed. With her pale skin, she never was able to hide her embarrassment, and not being able to use a writing utensil would've qualified. Thankfully, he'd instructed her in the same tone he'd sported since they'd gotten in this room. She did as he said, signed the contract, and set the pen on top of it before pushing it toward Axle. Lorenzo had already signed his copy and was leaning back in his chair, waiting on her.

Axle picked up the paperwork and handed it to one of the men in the room without ever looking at him. He pocketed his fancy schmancy pen as his eyes stayed trained on her. "Now that that's outta the way, I'll show you to your barracks. Follow me."

She stood automatically and started toward the door, but when his words actually registered, she rocked back on her heels. "What?" she asked. *Barracks.* She didn't hear him right. Surely. Please, God, no.

He faced her and crossed his arms. "Twenty-four-seven, Caitlin. Where you go, I go. Where I go, they go," he said, nodding toward the men who stood in line behind her, waiting to exit the room. "Even though the hotel the press corps uses is as safe as to be expected around here, it's not on base. The military isn't going to shell out the funds to put all of us up for the duration of your stay. It's easier—and more strategic—to give you a room here."

Then, for the first time since meeting him, he smiled, and the action almost knocked the air out of her lungs. She would've gasped for breath if she didn't know she was physically fine and only mentally reacting to what she was seeing. She'd idly thought him hot earlier, but when the man smiled? Jeez, he transformed into some living god.

Too bad he had a cocky attitude to go along with his looks. Like it was a cosmic joke. Or maybe that was a good thing he had an attitude problem. Being hot didn't mean he was *attractive*. Only the whole package—looks and charm— could be that. Besides, she didn't need to let some sexy soldier distract her from her work, and if he was pleasant on top of gorgeous, she'd have a tough time keeping her eyes on her job and off him. "I understand."

Although, she didn't. She really didn't. This whole thing was completely complicated.

A ghost of a smile lingered on his face, and a wary feeling came over her.

"Don't worry, Caitlin. Just because there'll be two beds in your room doesn't mean I'm sleeping in there with you. *Every* night."

"*Huh?*" But she knew. There was a chance he'd be sleeping in there *some* nights.

The smile now made sense.

This prick would be really invading her personal space. He not only knew she wasn't going to be happy about it, but also delighted in her discomfort. At least his lips had slipped back to their normal flat position of stern indifference with her outburst, and that stupid sexy smile was gone. It was slowly becoming obvious to Caitlin she might never get a moment alone here. Besides hindering the very reason she was in this country in the first place, which would require her to do some things without him around, she needed a shower and some sleep. Things she definitely needed to do alone and had been looking forward to since stepping off the plane. She was going to have a fight on her hands for every moment of privacy. "This is bull—"

"I'll have a room right next to yours, so you will get some time to yourself," he said, cutting her off as if reading her thoughts. "Your room will have its own toilet, too, but we'll have to coordinate your shower time." He half-smiled, and if she wasn't irritated, she'd find it just as stunning. "Last thing I need is for one of these yahoos to stumble in accidentally." His gaze shot above her, and she knew he was staring down the troops. "Don't forget what I told you this morning about pulling any accidentally-on-purpose shit, too."

She jumped at the chorus of, "Sir, yes, sir," coming from behind.

"Jesus, warn a girl," she muttered over her shoulder.

"They don't take orders from you," Axle said.

"Whatever. Can we get this show on the road? I'm calling first dibs on the shower. And I need food and sleep." She hated verbalizing these things because she didn't want to come off as weak. No doubt the men in this room had gone days without showers, beds, or fresh food several times in their lives, and here she was, demanding them like a diva. By the time she left Afghanistan, she'd have a whole new appreciation for what the troops had to endure on deployments, and by no means would she be experiencing anything close to that. "Sorry if that came out wrong," she said after chastising herself.

She needed to accept this course of events quickly and learn to work with it, not against it...and by *it*, she meant Axle.

He watched her for several seconds, then looked up again. "Acker, get Ms. Cooper some chow."

She looked back as she heard a man's agreement to follow the order and watched as he left the room.

"It'll take him about forty minutes to get to the chow hall, secure your meal, and get to the barracks. That'll give you time to drop off your bags and shower first."

"Thank you," she breathed as her shoulders fell, relieving the tension she hadn't known she'd been showing. He turned to walk out, and she followed silently this time.

When they got outside, Lorenzo asked, "What time do I need to back here in the morning?"

Caitlin gaped at him.

"Oh-six," she heard Axle reply.

She lifted her hands. "Wait, wait, wait. He doesn't have to stay on base?"

Axle stared down at her, but his mouth stayed shut as if it was his right to answer her question and he'd chosen not to.

"The station has already paid for my room," Lorenzo said from beside her, and she tore her gaze away from Axle to look at the cameraman. "The military offered yesterday to provide the same accommodations to me, but no way am I giving up my own room and shower." He chuckled.

She couldn't blame him, and the fact that Lorenzo had been given a choice, and she hadn't was more proof Axle being here was Hunter's doing.

She wasn't sure if Hunter and Axle knew each other personally or not. If so, their connection happened after Hunter had grown up and moved off because Caitlin definitely would've remembered Axle if he was from their small hometown. Chances were Axle was a byproduct of Hunter's connections elsewhere. When she got back to the

States, she'd be getting the scoop on just exactly what her childhood crush had been up to in recent years, but she wouldn't be waiting until she got back to find out exactly what his connection to Axle was.

She could question Axle, but even weary from travel and hunger, she knew better than to ask him just yet. She needed more information from Hunter before she said anything to the brooding man she just met. He'd made his displeasure of this assignment abundantly clear.

Instead of harping on their accommodations further, she shook Lorenzo's hand, told him she looked forward to working with him, and watched him walk off with one of the military guys that had circled them.

Axle motioned her toward the ATV and she quietly got in.

The area of barracks wasn't far from where they'd signed the paperwork. Just barely far enough for her to renew her focus for this assignment. She'd get the information her station needed for a great story, prove she had the chops to handle the biggies, and push for an even juicer story to work on. The little pep talk was starting to work, too, until they pulled to a stop in front of the tiniest building she'd seen since landing, and more dread eased in. She hid her displeasure, hoping it was larger on the inside than it looked on the outside. Some sort of secret *go-go-gadget* military housing. She clung to hope, no matter how ridiculous that sounded even to her.

That hope evaporated when she walked inside. *Craaap.* No, cramped. That was the right word she was looking for. Caitlin could stand in the middle of the hall and almost touch every door visible.

At least she had her own room. *Semi-private*, she added silently.

Axle gave her a quick tour...quick because it literally only took about thirty seconds. The guys in the group were bunking two to each room and they departed to their assigned bunks. Axle had his own room, but the second bed would be available for Lorenzo when he needed to stay on base. Once inside her room, Axle stood at the door.

"Take the bed on the left. The right is closer to the door. It keeps me between you and any danger."

Danger from what? Thousands of US military in the middle of a heavily armed base? She kept those thoughts to herself.

"Shower's across the hall. I put you in this room because it's closest to it and if anyone comes into the barracks, they have to get past four other rooms of trained military men."

She nodded as she looked around, taking in the sparse room.

"Caitlin?"

She glanced up at Axle, almost stunned at the soft murmur of her name coming from the hardened special ops man.

"I know this isn't ideal. For *either* of us," he added with a slight smile. "But you're in safe hands with me." Then he squared his shoulders and said all business-like, "Eat, shower, rest. We leave at oh-six."

It was midday, and she really needed to get working on her story after a quick nap. It would take days to get over her jet lag, so she would be sleeping in spurts until her body adjusted.

She couldn't think beyond the next thirty minutes right now, though. She gave him a nod, and then, for added fun, she flopped her hand to her forehead and said, "Sir, yes, sir." But her words held none of the sharp retort of a trained person.

He shook his head almost in amusement. "We'll work on that."

When he turned to leave, she sat on the bed and shut her eyes on a deep inhale. Learning to salute properly was at the end of her agenda.

CHAPTER THREE

Axle heard Caitlin rummaging around in her room as he stood outside her door the next morning. After he'd left her in her room last night, she'd unpacked, showered, ate, and crashed just as he suspected she would. The woman had been dead on her feet by the time they'd arrived at the barracks. When discussing the room assignment, he'd purposely led her to believe they could be sleeping in the same room. It hadn't necessarily been true. Anything was possible, sure, but he hoped it wouldn't come to that. Regardless, he fully intended to come and go as he pleased to check on her, and he didn't need her thinking she could shut him out of the room on a whim. She was under his protection, and if he determined they needed to be hunkered down in the same room at some point, it was better she understood that on the front end.

He'd also sent up a silent thank you for the cameraman choosing not to accept the military accommodations offered to him. If he had, the man would be sharing a room with Axle since he couldn't have the guy bunking with one of the soldiers and disrupting the buddy system he'd put in place. He'd been given six men as part of this assignment, which he grouped into pairs. The men would be his backup where Caitlin was concerned, but they'd also be responsible for driving them to their locations and engaging any hostiles. As much as Burge had put the responsibility of Caitlin's safety on his shoulders, he knew he'd be SOL if he took her—and by association, the videographer—out into the red zone on his own. No one traveled out there alone. He'd needed a team of competent men he could entrust her safety with. Burge had made some calls and secured Axle six recent BUD/S graduates. These men had survived the intensive twenty-four week course, and the infamous Hell Week. Axle couldn't suppress a shudder at remembering when he'd gone through it. But these guys still had to go through parachute jump school, and then complete the longest course—SEAL Qualification Training—before wearing their Navy Seal Trident and being assigned to their own SEAL team.

Immediately after looking up who this reporter was, Axle had to tamp down some renewed anger at being assigned this mission. She wasn't some big hotshot war correspondent or high-profile news anchor. She was practically a nobody.

Frustrated, he'd checked his messages. A few members of his SEAL team had razed him for being assigned this urinal duty of an assignment, and he couldn't blame them. If one of them had gotten this op, he'd have done the same. His sister had also sent him a message. "Don't hate me." That could be any number of things. He knew she was dealing with a lot after being shot. He was being a shitty brother, not making more time to talk to her. Once he got a handle on this new arrangement he was in, he'd reach out to her. Right now, he had to do more digging on his new charge.

He'd only found a few pieces on YouTube of Caitlin's reports from bases. One of them had even spelled her name wrong. Looking her up hadn't pointed to any significant reason why she in particular—out of all the news correspondents he'd been around on deployment—required SEAL protection. Not that he wished her any harm. He wasn't a monster. But learning there really wasn't more to what Burge told him about her hadn't set well with him. She was of no importance, which meant her protection truly had been secured by someone cashing in a favor.

That knowledge had burned at a low simmer.

What cranked up the heat had been realizing just how beautiful and *fair* she was. He'd watched her piece from Kandahar so many times that he could recite the questions she asked of the soldier. Learning all about her had been part of his preparation, but seeing that pale blonde hair, light blue eyes, and alabaster skin had him wondering how in the hell she was going to blend in. She screamed *American*, and a bombshell at that.

Not that her looks mattered to him. Another place, another time, he would totally hit on her, and Axle was confident enough to know when he wanted something, he usually got it. But never once had he fraternized with colleagues, and he sure as hell wasn't going to do something as stupid as that with a woman he'd been charged with protecting.

The door opened and she walked out wearing cargo pants, boots, a tank, and an open shirt over it. He almost groaned at the sight of her. Not that it would've been a completely sexual response.

"You need to cover up," he said without letting his gaze

leave hers. He didn't have to look at her body to see her curves were on display. Most straight, red-blooded American men his age knew how to check out a woman's rack without getting caught. It was a skill he'd picked up long before entering the Navy.

"And here I thought the first words outta your mouth would be an apology for us getting off on the wrong foot yesterday. You know, encourage a new day, fresh start, sorta thing."

Apologize? For doing his job? He briefly squeezed his eyes shut. "I'm sorry."

"Now was that so hard?" She giggled, but stopped quickly. "Oh, I brought a scarf," she said, digging into her bag and pulling the edge of a hijab out for him to see.

"No, Caitlin, though I'm glad you thought of that." He ran a hand through his hair. He needed a cut, but being special ops, he didn't have to live with the same military regulations. It was more important that he blend in with his surroundings than sport a high and tight. If Caitlin was military, she'd have her locks pulled back and not flowing freely, so she had the right idea here, but was focusing on addressing the wrong thing. "I mean your shirt."

She gasped and looked down. "What's wrong with my shirt?" she asked, obviously confused, but he detected a hint of anger in her response as well.

"Besides the fact that your skin is so pale that you should cover as much of it as possible to protect it from the *desert*?" he asked sarcastically, though it hadn't really been a question. "You're in a country where women are usually covered. I want you to blend in, not stand the fuck out." He hadn't meant to cuss, but he was warring with himself as much as he was her. He didn't want her to cover her beautiful body. The fact he felt that way and that he had to ask her to block herself from his view pissed him off on competing levels. She had nothing to do with what was going on in his head. But then there was the fact she should know better than to venture out like this. Granted, this would be her first assignment outside the wire, but she'd been in this country before. Even if she hadn't or worked in the media, she would've seen images of the women here.

Her cheeks turned pink, and he immediately regretted causing her any embarrassment. "It's just so hot. I thought maybe the scarf would help cover me when I had to wear it."

He took a deep breath and stepped toward her. Only one, though. He kept his arms crossed as he looked down at her and did his best to temper his words. "It's okay. This is new, and it's hot as hell. But I'd rather you be sweating and miserable than cool and killed."

She nodded, dropped the bag she'd brought out with her, and darted back into her room. He checked his watch, but he didn't have to wait long. She emerged less than a minute later wearing a long-sleeve, fitted t-shirt. He wanted to howl because, somehow, without the blanket of the loose button-up shirt she'd worn over the tank top, she was on display even more. That damn cotton clung to her like a second skin. *Jesus.*

She spread her arms. "How do I look?"

Like a sinful siren. "Better. Follow me," he barked, and turned on his heels without another glance. He heard her heft the bag before she shuffled behind him out of the barracks.

"We didn't get a chance to talk yesterday about the agenda."

"You were dead on your feet," he said without looking at her. "I'd just have to go through it all again this morning."

She harrumphed, and he was glad she couldn't see the flash of his grin. "I'm all ears, soldier."

"Technically, I'm in the Navy. Makes me a sailor."

"If I call you sailor, that'll make me feel like I'm reciting some cheesy line in a porno." She snorted. "Well, hello there, sailor. Let me raise that big, hard anchor of yours," she said in a sultry tone that had his cock stirring. He stopped suddenly, and she ran into his back. "*Oaf.*"

He turned and clasped her shoulders to steady her. Caitlin's eyes were huge as she stared up at him, startled. She'd been joking with him, but no way did she know just how much he wanted to take her up on that teasing offer. He opened his mouth to tell her—what? What was he going to say? Any reprimand died on his tongue as he gazed down at her. He immediately let go and turned before he did something stupid, not giving his brain a chance to send any dangerous commands to his hands or mouth, and then marched out of the building.

He climbed into the driver's side of the Hummer and waited for her to get seated. Before she had a chance to brace herself, he peeled out, heading for the airstrip. Determined to keep his mind on his job of protecting her body, and not exploiting it, he said, "It'd take us half a day to drive to the Achin District, not to mention the road is one of the most dangerous in the world. A helo will take us to Jalalabad, and we're driving from there. It'll cut travel time in half."

"Why not take the helicopter all the way?"

It was a good question, not that he liked having his decisions second-guessed. "We will after today. You've been cleared to interview some of the units on the ground, and we need to get that out of the way first. It'll be easier to drive among them. Tomorrow, we'll take the helo over the actual bombsight and surrounding areas to give you a lay of the land and aerial footage. The next several days after that, we'll fly to a specific quadrant and land, so you can walk in the designated area, meet locals—*friendly* locals—before heading back to base for the night. Each day, we'll fly to a different quadrant so you can investigate and film whatever it is you're interested in seeing until you've put eyes on everything."

She was silent, and he gripped the wheel tighter when the urge to keep talking bubbled up.

"I'm sorry for earlier."

"Nothing to apologize for," he said automatically. If either of them owed the other an apology, it was him for reacting to her words at all.

"It was inappropriate. You're here to protect me. I insulted you. And I went through that whole thing about expecting an apology from you. I can't expect you to do that if I can't even—"

"You didn't insult me."

"Yes, I did."

"Let it go, Caitlin," he said in the tone he reserved for his subordinates because he didn't want her to say those words again, or worse, elaborate on them. When he glanced at her to make sure she understood how serious he was about this, his gut clenched at the sight of her red cheeks. She really did feel bad thinking she'd offended him. He hated that, but to entertain this conversation further was to invite unnecessary danger...and not the battlefield kind.

"Sir, yes, sir," she said with flimsy salute before looking out the side window. Thank God she dropped it, but that salute? He really needed to correct her form if she kept doing it.

Later. He'd have to do it later. Right now, he needed to

take advantage of the quiet to get his head straight. They were heading into enemy territory, and he wouldn't let anything get in his way of protecting her.

Not her. And especially not him.

————

"THE FOOD TASTES LIKE DIRT," Lorenzo said after they landed. A couple of Axle's men left to secure the cars they'd be taking, and Axle had instructed them to eat since the chow hall hadn't been fully up by the time they had to leave base. Caitlin had packed some energy bars, so she hadn't planned on eating, but Axle hadn't wanted to hear her explanation when she tried to decline. The man didn't like it when she questioned or resisted him.

"It tastes like dirt made a baby with dirt and gave birth to more dirt," she added as she choked down another spoonful. "They take *dirty rice* a little too literally over here."

Lorenzo chuckled. "I think you're gonna fit it in quite nicely, Caitlin. Hard to survive this kind of assignment with your sense of humor still intact."

She scooped some more rice, but then dropped it and pushed her plate away, giving up the battle that her taste buds would find anything in the food beyond marginally edible. "Thanks. How long have you been here?"

His gaze darkened. "Off and on for ten years."

"Oh," she said, unable to wrap her mind around that. "Do you have family back home?"

He pushed his empty plate away with a shrug. "Where's home?" he asked, but she didn't think he expected an answer. "I was born in Rome. Moved to London when I was eight. And went to university in America. I've worked on every continent."

"So no wife and kids?"

He laughed. "Who has time for that? My American friends would say things about picket fences and the American Dream. Whatever that is." He shook his head dismissively. "My life is work."

She felt a little sad at the way he'd said that. "Do you ever just take off and relax?"

He half smiled. "Actually, I was due for holiday when Jack called. He sent Kanfi with Harris to Syria. After the station budget cuts, the executives frown on paying freelancers. He could have gotten someone else, but it would've taken time he hadn't wanted to waste."

"The news never sleeps."

He laughed. "Oh heavens, does he still use that phrase?"

"Jack is nothing if not routine."

"Time to go," Axle said from behind her. She looked over her shoulder and watched as he approached, knowing he stood off to the side to let her eat, but not letting her out of his site. But, this time, he wasn't looking at her. His gaze was locked on Lorenzo. She faced her colleague, but he seemed oblivious he was on the receiving end of a murderous glare as he moved to get up from the table. Caitlin grabbed her plate and stood to toss it.

Axle clutched her wrist and she gasped, not expecting him to be standing right there when she got up. His lack of personal space unsettled her...more than it should.

"You didn't eat," he muttered.

"It's gross." It was true, but saying it out loud made her feel like a snob. She was nothing of the sort. Caitlin prided herself on her modesty and had eaten local cuisine from many places, even ones squeamish people would balk at. Not once had she complained about what she'd been served. Hell, even if it was something she wouldn't ordinarily eat—like crickets—she'd been more worried about offending the people around her than her own comfort. But it was different with Axle. She didn't have to hide anything with him.

"Caitlin," he said, and briefly shut his eyes. "You have to eat. If you don't, you'll be too weak to run away from danger."

She reached for him, grabbed his free arm. "I tried to tell you earlier I have energy bars with me."

He didn't say anything, and it dawned on her that she was holding his arm as he was hers, as if they were almost in an embrace. In a country where public display of affection was forbidden, she should be worried how this looked to the people around them. But since this area was filled with coalition forces who were used to seeing people doing a lot more in their home countries, maybe it wouldn't come off as offensive to anyone.

Because as much as she told herself to let go of him, her hand refused to follow the order.

His throat moved, and in his gaze was something she'd seen for a fleeting moment once before, but this time it lingered, leaving no question what had been banked there then or now. Heat. Desire.

Axle wanted her.

Her heart quickened with the knowledge. From thrill? Fear? As she stared back, she knew the answer. Both. She was both excited and scared by this, by what he stirred within her. He had an enigmatic sense about him. Strong, confident, mysterious. This kind of reaction was not like her. At. All. She was sensible...when her college friends had been partying, she had her nose in a book. When colleagues were online shopping at work, she was researching the next story. The only part of her body she let dictate anything in her life was her brain. Right now, it was screaming at her that she didn't know this man. Hunter never told her anything about the person who'd be protecting her. Axle could be married, for goodness sakes.

"If you two are done making goo-goo eyes at each other," Lorenzo said from beside them, and they both immediately dropped their hands.

"What?" Axle said low and dark. If voices alone could kill someone, his would have murdered Lorenzo right there on the spot.

Lorenzo took a step back. "Um, I was just going to say those men you sent for the car are back."

Axle stormed off to where the soldiers where gathered.

"Damn, that was intense."

"Yeah," she breathed, though she was positive Lorenzo had been talking about how Axle reacted toward him, and not the moment the two of them had just shared.

What the hell was she doing? She could not get a crush on the military muscle. She was here to do a job and the last thing she wanted to do was get distracted, or worse— compromise her story.

When Axle returned, he was all business, and she was relieved. He directed them to the car and assisted them as they loaded their gear before coming toward her.

She instinctively backed up.

Her back hit the vehicle.

He cocked an eyebrow at her as if to ask just where she was going, but thankfully, he kept his mouth shut. He lifted his hand, showing her the helmet she'd had earlier, almost if chastising her for forgetting it.

"I knew where it was." She didn't, and she blamed what happened just a moment ago for the reason. Instead of handing it to her this time, though, he slipped it on her head and helped her with it. If her breath quickened at the feel of him tucking her hair in the hijab, or his finger grazing her chin, she ignored it. He opened the door and lifted her to the seat in the back.

She gasped at his sudden movement and his tough-man strength. But his breathing never even changed, nor did he show any signs whatsoever of exertion. She wasn't a big lady, but she was on a first-name basis with the carhops at Sonic. *Strawberry cheesecake milkshake, please and thank you!* She looked like a blonde version of one of the Kardashian women, just not the model-thin one. Having his hands on her waist, even briefly, was almost too much for her to control. She lifted her hand and placed it on his shoulder to keep distance between them and help balance herself as she sucked in her tummy. It was instinct, she told herself. But touching him as he touched her only ignited this foreign longing she felt. Whatever was happening with him was happening too fast and was too foreign to her to put a name on. She'd never had this kind of a response to any man. None. And she'd been in the same room as Jason Momoa when working on her thesis project.

To hide her body's reaction, she quipped, "I thought ladies get to ride shotgun."

"You are," he said as he pointed to a hole in the roof where a machine gun was. She covered her mouth in shock and looked at him. His pinched lips and the gleam in his eyes told her he was fighting a smile.

"That's not what I mean."

"But that's what you get."

"Really?" she asked, and looked at the space again.

He sobered. "Can't have anyone seeing you through the windshield and taking shots. You're sitting here because I'm riding passenger and can watch you from the corner of my eye."

"I don't think twenty-four-seven actually means you have to sit with your eyeballs glued to my body."

He leaned closer and she sunk back into the seat to maintain space. It didn't work. He reached over her, dug around for something out of her view, and softly said, "There aren't many perks to this job—" He pulled out a breakfast sandwich and handed it to her—"Getting to look at you isn't the hardship here."

She opened her mouth, stunned by his words, but he shut the door before she could say anything. Once he was seated in his own spot, he glanced at her, and she was sure her mouth hung open still. "Eat. Save the energy bars for emergencies."

They headed out, and she stared at the biscuit with egg enveloped in plastic wrap. She hadn't seen anything like this as an option, only rice, so where had he gotten it? She looked beside her seat and discovered he'd been rummaging around in his own backpack. This had been *his* breakfast, and he was giving it to her.

Her heart stuttered as warmth filled her. This man who she hardly knew, who'd been hired to protect her, was sacrificing his own comfort to make sure she ate something she liked. The gesture might not seem big, but it was probably one of the nicest things anybody had done for her. The act was one she'd never forget...even if she couldn't accept it. She pushed the sandwich toward him.

"Thank you, but I can't take your food. You lectured me on having energy to run from bad guys. Can't have you passing out from low blood sugar in the middle of shooting people."

He raised an eyebrow, and the gesture had been as sexy

as the last time he'd done it. Several seconds passed before he spoke. When he did, his words came out slow, distinct. "You have no idea of the years of training my body's been through. I can go without food, water, and sleep for periods of time that a lesser person would die from."

Her hand dropped slightly, but she didn't say anything. What could she? She knew the military didn't skimp on training. She had no doubt as to what he'd just said.

"You will eat that sandwich. If we were the only two Westerners in this country, that sandwich the only food left behind, and it came down to you or me eating it, it'd still be all you."

"Well, now you're just being silly," she said as she eased back from his level stare and opened it. If he wasn't going to take it, she wasn't going to make him. She was hungry and it did smell delicious.

He chuckled, and she decided she liked the sound of his laugh. "Sweetheart, you're no good to me weak."

She knew the endearment hadn't been literal, but her cheeks grew warm anyway. Best thing for her to do was ignore the man in front and be grateful she had something pleasant to munch on.

He confused her, twisted her in ways that she'd never been before, and *never* so quickly after meeting someone.

She wished she understood why this man in particular did that to her...almost as much as she wished he had no effect on her at all.

Almost.

CHAPTER FOUR

THEY'D BEEN on the road for about an hour with Axle keeping constant watch of their surroundings. They'd stopped several times to investigate possible IEDs, but so far, it had been all clear. That didn't stop Axle from scanning for any anomalies, though.

He'd hated to take his gaze off the landscape even for a second, but he had to in order to glance at Caitlin. She'd gone quiet after he'd given her the breakfast sandwich. It had been maddening when she'd tried refusing the food he'd offered. It was another example of her not following his orders without question. But if he was completely honest, it had also been sweet of her since she'd done it thinking he hadn't eaten anything that morning. He had, of course. He'd had some chow brought to him last night while she'd been sleeping and had asked for some easily transported breakfast for him and Caitlin for this morning since they had to leave around the time the chow hall opened. It would've been packed, and they wouldn't have had time to eat and get in the air on schedule. He heated the four sandwiches this morning, scarfing down two and packing the others right before she was scheduled to meet up with him. He'd had every intention of telling her first thing, but when she'd walked out with a low-cut tank top, his brain scrambled. Then she'd gone and dropped that porno bit, and all logic was MIA. They were in the air when he remembered, and by the time they landed in Jalalabad, he knew her breakfast wouldn't be warm anymore. It was the reason he'd wanted her to eat something hot before loading up in the ground transport. It hadn't worked. He should've given her the cold eggs anyway. After she'd stopped protesting, she'd inhaled it as if it was the best meal she'd ever eaten.

When finished, she'd pulled out her laptop and started working. She'd asked questions every once in a while to Lorenzo who sat in the back with her. How to spell certain words after muttering what Axle thought were cuss words before groaning about not having Internet. He couldn't be sure since it wasn't exactly quiet in this ride.

"What's the name of the unit you said we're visiting first?" she asked.

Axle's gaze blinked at her on autopilot, but this time she looked at him instead of her work partner, asking Axle directly. "I didn't." He looked back out the windshield.

"Is it classified?"

"No," he answered with another look, keeping his focus on her this time.

She squinted at him. "Are you being evasive on purpose?"

"Yes."

"Why?" she asked slowly with a tilt of her head.

He was just messing with her. He didn't know why he liked giving her a hard time. Normally, he was helpful and forthcoming with information. Well, information that wasn't classified, and if anything surrounding these units was, he wouldn't be taking her to see them. He also knew his orders, so he wouldn't be any of her information sources. But this wasn't the same thing.

"Because you're a journalist. It's your job to uncover the truth, not have it spoon fed to you." He winked to lighten the punch of his words, but he immediately regretted that almost involuntary action. Her cheeks grew pink, and he got a knot in his stomach as he resisted the urge to stroke them.

What the fuck? Where in the world was this need to comfort this woman coming from? He sure as hell couldn't touch her like that. The few times he'd had his hands on her had electrified him to the point he'd had to wade through the lusty fog of his brain to find his professional ethics. He's only known her inside of twenty-hour hours. There was no reason for this kind of response to her. With each touch, it was getting harder and harder to keep his distance. And that wasn't the only thing getting hard.

Maybe he'd been on tour too long. Yeah, that had to be it.

"I'm doing my job by asking you."

"I'm not authorized to answer your questions." It was the truth, and she needed to know it. Granted, the order Burge had given him didn't really apply to this scenario. It was military data Axle couldn't share, not their agenda. His responsibility to keep her safe meant he could choose to share relevant information at the last possible moment, and he couldn't help stalling just a little longer.

"But I need—"

"The 39th Infantry Brigade, A Company, 28th Signal," the man driving said at the same time, stopping her from finishing her statement.

"Acker," Axle barked. "Did I give you permission to speak on my fucking behalf?"

The man stiffened. "No, sir!"

Axle rubbed a hand over his face to get his wits about him and looked at Caitlin. She was typing away on her keyboard, probably noting the name of the unit. He sighed and then said, "We're visiting the servicemen of the 39th Infantry Brigade out of Arkansas first. Then we'll meet up with the 1st Calvary Division Sustainment Brigade." He hesitated before adding, "They're both army units."

"Thank you," she said as she kept typing. When she finished, she looked up, "What did you mean you're not authorized to answer my questions?"

"I'm here to protect you. That's it."

"But you're stationed here." She frowned. "You have an inside perspective that I don't."

"Doesn't mean I'm going to provide specifics."

She huffed, not that he could hear it. "My boss is not going to be happy about this. I have a job to do."

"Me, too. And *my* boss isn't allowing me to speak to you on the record. Guarantee you, he's a hell of a lot more intimidating than yours."

Her mouth fell open, and he could tell her brain was processing that little bit of information. "But you could tell me general information without giving up any details. That's what he's worried about, right?"

"I'm your guard, not Google."

She glared at him. "That's not what I mean."

"I know." He shrugged. "But aside from your personal wellbeing and your agenda, you need to direct your questions to the people authorized to discuss this with you."

"ETA ten minutes, sir," Acker said.

Axle turned and checked his rifle and sidearm as he said, "Be ready to dive right in when we get there, Caitlin. We have an hour with each team, no more."

He heard her rustling around and looked to see what she was doing. She'd packed her laptop and pulled out a notebook.

"Crap," she muttered as she kept digging in her bag. "I can't find my pen."

Axle pulled his favorite tactical pen out and handed it to her. It was the same one he'd handed to her when she'd signed the paperwork. He never let anyone use. Even when he was on leave, he had it with him. "I'm going to start charging you to use this thing."

She glowered at him, but took it. "Put it on my—"

A crack split the air. It was an all too familiar sound. No matter how prepared he was, no matter the armor surrounding him, it would always give him nightmares. "Get down!" he yelled, cutting her off.

He had his assault rifle on the ready and yanked it up, searching for the shooter who'd popped one off at them. He was relieved Caitlin had immediately buried her head between her knees.

"Came in from the east," Acker barked, and swerved the vehicle from side to side, making it more difficult for the person to get another shot at them. If they were still in the crosshairs, the zigzagging would make it much more difficult for the enemy to hit them.

Axle pushed the button on his comm. "Haverty? You got eyes on the shooter?"

Several more shots rang out, sounding too close. Way too fucking close. Axle cussed out loud, and at the same time, Haverty replied, "Negative, sir. Team is scoping."

That meant the guys in the other vehicle had their binoculars out, looking. Axle would have done the same, but his main focus was Caitlin. He glanced at her again, and she was visibly shaking. He reached out to pat her knee, hoping to ease her fears if only just slightly.

He looked out the side and saw a flash from a rifle before a shot whizzed right by, ricocheting off a boulder they'd just passed. Shit, that was way too close! But at least it clued him in on the direction the attack was coming from. He aimed in that vicinity and fired several times. The vehicle came to a screeching stop right as Acker called the others with the location of where the hit had come. Within seconds, Axle wasn't the only one pelting the area with rounds of ammo. He ceased and swung his focus around the front and other side since his guys had the other direction handled. When he was certain no fire came from anywhere else, he dropped his rifle. The others had stopped shooting, and they all sat silently, listening. Caitlin breathed heavily, but Axle couldn't look at her again just yet. When he felt confident they weren't under attack any longer, he pressed his comm and said, "Let's move. We'll do a battle damage assessment when we get there."

He checked his rifle as they surged forward with the momentum of the speeding vehicle.

"That's never happened to me before," Lorenzo said, not even trying to hide the panic in his voice.

"We were lucky," Axle said flatly. "Couldn't have been more than a couple of guys out there. Could've been a lot more." There usually was, but he didn't want to say that.

He twisted to the side. Caitlin still had her head between her legs, so he reached over and rubbed the one closest to him. "You can sit up now."

She trembled under his hand, and he hated she was scared, but damn, they were in a war zone. It was a rare day around here when he wasn't getting shot at. It was the very reason he didn't agree with journalists being embedded in any unit. The cost of causalities was too great.

Slowly, she rose, her eyes wide. He had this insane urge to pull her into his lap and coddle her. Of course, he couldn't, but more importantly, he hated the fact his instinct was to do just that.

It's because you have to protect her, that's all.

He didn't believe the lie one bit, nor did he like just how aware he was she sparked something within him.

"Caitlin, you're okay," he said slowly. Her head jerked around as if she was a cornered animal. His hand on her leg had stilled, so he stroked her gently again. "Hey, there. Look at me."

She did and her mouth opened, working as if to say something. He waited patiently for her to get whatever it was out. "S-sorry," she said, her voice cracking. She shook her head as if clearing it and took a deep breath. "Sorry," she said a little more confidently this time.

A surge of pride filled him at her willingness to be brave in a circumstance he was quite sure she'd never experienced before.

"Don't apologize. You did what you were told." He smiled at her.

"Now if only you'd mind me when you're *not* being shot at," he said, trying to help her relax. The danger wasn't over. It never would be, but the immediate threat had been neutralized.

She shuttered her eyes, and unlike before, he was glad to see the spark of her defiance. "This is different."

That was true, and it'd do her well to be reminded of that often—verbally—so that she wouldn't be too shocked to react whenever reality took aim at them again. "Exactly.

This is a war zone, Caitlin. Shots can be fired at anytime, anywhere."

She sucked in another breath and nodded. He didn't like her learning this lesson so explicitly, but if it took a couple of tangos on a roadside to drive the point home, then so be it.

He just hoped that was the only time he'd have to shield her from gunfire. He'd been very meticulous in planning the absolute safest agenda he could. He was pretty sure whoever attacked them just happened to be at the right place at the right time. Not that it mattered. He'd have to reevaluate his plans and make modifications.

He really didn't want to take on any other insurgents without his team. His brothers. He was pleased how quickly these new guys reacted. Still, he wasn't used to working alongside them. And Caitlin? She was a complete wildcard. No military training at all, focusing more on her work than on her surroundings. Whoever called in that favor knew what they were doing. Because she had no idea exactly what she'd just stepped into, and Axle was now duty-bound to protect her.

And he would. But he'd gladly stand in the line of fire and take a bullet for her. The understanding did something funny to his chest, so he let go of her leg and faced the front, hoping the physical disconnect would help. Yeah, getting shot would hurt, but the knowledge that she could be injured—or worse—fucking hurt him in a different way... and not touching didn't help that reality at all.

If he didn't get a handle on whatever the fuck she was doing to him, it wouldn't matter if he did get taken out. He'd be toast anyway.

CHAPTER FIVE

CAITLIN WAS STILL RATTLED by the time they'd made it back to base that evening. She was a professional, so she'd done her job, interviewed the soldiers in the field, asked them about their knowledge of the MOAB dropped in Nangarhar. None of them had said anything to make her think there was some cover-up or more going on outside of what NATO had stated in the press release following the air strike. Of course, that didn't mean much. The intel could be outside of their job scopes, or it could even be classified. She needed to get in the field and question the locals. They wouldn't have to understand specific military dynamics to know if something was up. If there were men with guns trekking around in the days before and after the air strike, chances were someone saw something. People didn't forget experiencing something like that firsthand. Even what seemed only inconsequential to a bystander could be something of major importance to her story.

For about the hundredth time today, visions of what happened earlier flashed through her mind. She'd known there was a risk she'd get shot at. It had been a lecture her father and Hunter had given her. In addition to her boss. Even Heather had tried warning her. But knowing it was possible and it actually happening—the first time out, no less—were two completely different things.

She wanted to call Heather. Actually, she wanted to talk to Hunter, but she didn't have another way to reach him. He'd been the one to instigate her protection, so she wanted to find out just how he knew Axle. After what happened today, that information held even more importance, and she wasn't even thinking about how he'd made her heart race. Oh, that had been the initial reason she'd wanted to find out. No mistaking that, but that knowledge carried more importance after getting shot at.

Even with her head between her knees, Caitlin could sense nothing but calm efficiency from Axle. He'd been quick. Possibly even deadly. She had no idea if any reconnaissance team went out to investigate the area and look for bodies, or if something like that was chalked up to the battles of war with no importance placed on whether or not any enemy forces survived the return of fire. She could see both sides of the argument when she looked at it objectively. That meant, he could have easily killed someone and not know it. Realistically, she knew that was a product of war; she'd just never been up close and personal with that aspect, which was why it was extremely hard to wrap her head around it when her life almost became a statistic.

She reached for her laptop. Satellite calls were limited anyway and there was a nine-and-a-half-hour time difference. Surely Hunter was on social media. If she found him, she could send him a message now or have his info ready to try a video chat with him first thing in the morning. She searched all the major platforms. Nothing. The man was either too paranoid to put his personal information on the

World Wide Web, or he had his profiles completely locked down. Either was an honest possibility. She even looked at Heather's list of friends on Facebook and didn't see anybody named Hunter.

Not getting anywhere with Hunter, she decided to send Heather a message that she wanted to talk to her brother. It was too early in Arkansas to do a live chat right now. At least sending a message would get the ball rolling, and hopefully with minimal back-and-forth, she could set up a time for a video call with Hunter.

After opening up messenger, she saw Maya's name in a group chat the three of them had several months ago—the last time Caitlin rescheduled a girls' weekend.

Maya. New energy ignited in her. Maya wasn't just Heather's other best friend, she was Hunter's girlfriend. Caitlin understood how Hunter might've kept his sister from linking anything to him online, but if his girlfriend wanted to splash his face all over social media, he probably didn't have much say in the matter. Besides the fact men tended to placate their significant others, she'd heard Maya had Hunter wrapped around her pinky. She could bat her lashes, and Hunter would give her whatever she wanted.

That was how it should be. Maya was a lucky woman, not only because she had a great guy who loved her unconditionally, but also because that man was Hunter.

She pulled up Maya's page and started scanning. Even if Maya had her page locked down, it wouldn't matter. The two of them were friends online, too. Caitlin would be able to see everything she'd posted.

Jackpot. There wasn't much, but there was a "Call Me Ishmael" tagged in one photo with a heart emoji. She hadn't seen Hunter in years, but she'd recognize him anywhere. She went to Ishmael's profile page, and it, too, was private.

She couldn't see anything but a profile picture of a whale. At first, she didn't understand the significance of the profile name, thinking it could just be completely random in an effort to keep from being tracked down. Maybe even something that only held meaning for Maya and Hunter? She didn't know, but one quick Internet search answered that question.

It was the first line of *Moby Dick*, which had been written by Herman Melville.

She could see a man likening any dick reference to having a large penis, but she knew something about Hunter he rarely shared.

Something he absolutely hated.

His first name was Herman. Odds were, this account belonged to Hunter.

She clicked the message icon, and started a brief text, informing him it was Caitlin, and that she wanted to talk as soon as he had a chance. She didn't provide any details in writing. Although she was pretty sure this was Hunter's account, she didn't want to jump to conclusions. Plus, there was no reason to type out a big long message if this wasn't an account he was active on.

With that thought, she navigated to Heather's page and sent her a message as well. If that wasn't Hunter she'd just contacted, Caitlin didn't want to waste precious time chasing down a dead lead. She informed Heather she needed to speak to her brother right away. Since she knew Heather was on the other end of this message, she didn't have to be careful with identifying her location. She went into details about the time zone and a few possible time slots she'd be available for video chat. First thing in the morning for her would be mid-afternoon for him. That might be too difficult for him since that timeframe would probably still put him working at the garage. If he chose to contact her when he woke up, she'd have to stay up late at night to make that work. That was fine. She'd do whatever she needed to talk to him and find out what he knew about Axle. Hopefully, that insight would help her cope with this sudden anxiety.

She had every right to be freaked out, though. She'd been shot at!

How could she push the fear away and do her job when she couldn't make it one day without fearing for her life? Her feelings of death were valid, but if she was completely honest, it wasn't just concern for her own life that worried her. What would happen if the men she was with were injured or killed? What would she do then? Away from base with no one to protect her...

Suddenly, the rule about her not being able to carry a weapon seemed damned ridiculous.

She had retreated to her room under the guise of work, unable to face Axle after him seeing her act all scared. She'd thrown herself into her job and pretended it hadn't happened in order to get through the rest of the day. But now, he was just the man she needed to see.

She yanked her door open, intending to cross the hall and bang on his door, but his had already been opened. She hadn't had time to cross the distance to his room when he'd shot up and rushed to her.

"Where are you going?" he asked, standing tall and commanding right in front of her. His quiet speed stunned her.

"I...er...was coming to see you."

His shoulders relaxed, but air of authority wafted around him. "Good. I don't have to remind you that if you intend on exiting this building, I have to be with you."

She glared at him. "Then why did you just remind me?"

He huffed out a sigh. "Just making sure you get that."

"I'm not twelve." There was no need to patronize her.

He smiled in a way that warmed her insides, and gave her a momentary sense of calm. "No. You're definitely not." Just as quick as the smile appeared, it was gone. "What do you want?" he asked, all business, and any minor relaxation she'd felt had disappeared too.

She almost lost her nerve, but this was too serious. It wasn't just her life she had to worry about. It was her survival. "A gun."

He blinked. "I'm sorry, what?"

"I want a gun. After what happened today—" He started shaking his head, and it irritated her, but she continued anyway. "I think it's stupid for me not—"

"No," he said, slicing his hand through the air, forcing her to stop. "Don't even go there. I already told you that's not possible. If you carry a gun, you're considered a combatant and then anybody can come after you."

"Are you kidding me? No, really. I think it's pretty freaking clear I'll be shot at whether or not I'm packing."

He ran a hand through his short hair as a low groan escaped. "I get that today was scary—"

"That's not the point," she snapped, and almost stomped her foot. Thank God she didn't because it would've totally negated the whole, *I'm not twelve* defense. "It's dangerous out there. What if we get separated—"

"Won't happen."

"What if everyone gets blown up, and I'm left to defend myself?" she said, wanting him to grasp where this panic was coming from. On an intellectual level, she understood the rule, but it wasn't as if she could call foul and get special treatment from the big bad terrorists.

"Caitlin, you're letting your fear control your emotions."

"Damn right I am." She was breathing heavy. She knew this was a long shot, but she had to make him understand how important it was to her. She glanced around as panic settled over her. "I have to be able to defend myself if you are captured...or, or, or worse...have body parts scattered all over the place." Oh God, she was going to be sick...or pass out...or—

He grabbed her shoulders, and she gasped. "Caitlin."

She shook her head. She was going to hyperventilate.

"Take a deep breath." She tried, but it was shallow. He ordered her to do it again. "C'mon. Breathe with me, now."

She watched his lips and tried timing her breaths with his. Her lungs burned, but she did it.

"That's better," he whispered as he released her.

Her face flamed with embarrassment. Why was she even *on* this assignment if she couldn't handle the risks? She squeezed her eyes shut, not knowing what to say or what to do at this point. Not even a gun dealer in Texas would give her a firearm after how she just acted.

"The first time I got shot at," he said, and she opened her eyes. He'd leaned back against the wall, the most relaxed she'd ever seen him. "One of the men in my unit got killed."

"Wow." She watched him as he seemed to go to another place mentally. She was sure wherever it was, it was a lot grimmer than today.

"I went back to base and got drunk. It's not really advised, but it was either find the bottom of a bottle or find someone to beat up. Fight or flight instinct's a bitch when you can't actually flee." He blinked at her, seeming to come back to the presence. "Going through that? It's real, and it's raw, darlin'. Believe me, I know what you're feeling."

She was calmer now, and for that she was glad, but it didn't change her reality. Hopefully now she had her wits about her to articulate it better. "The difference, Axle, is you *know* how to fight. I don't. You're skilled in combat, which is awesome, but you also have help." She waved her hands at him. "You don't have that big rifle on you right now, but I see a gun on your leg. I bet you have other weapons, too. A knife? I have *nothing* to defend myself with."

He studied her for a long, agonizing minute. Then he jerked his head to the side. "Let's go."

She followed him outside.

"Hop in," he said after walking to an ATV.

"Where are we going?" she asked as she climbed in.

"You'll see."

They drove down the dirt road and pulled up next to what looked like a target range. She hadn't had time for a complete tour of the base, so she couldn't be sure. "We're shooting?" she asked, a smile forming slowly. If so, did that mean he was going to show her how to shoot a gun and let her carry one around? She'd never shot one before. *Probably need to keep that little bit of info to myself.*

Axle got out and she didn't wait for him to tell her to follow. If he was going to get her a weapon, she wanted to do it before he changed his mind. When she got to the front of the ATV, he grabbed her hand and tugged her behind him to the side of the area, moving quickly. She ignored her heart's sudden spike at his touch and blamed it on adrenaline of getting to fire a weapon.

"In a minute."

He turned to face her and placed his hands on her shoulders, staring down into her eyes.

Unable to take the silence, she darted her gaze around and asked, "What's going on?"

"You made a good point—"

"Yay—"

"In case I become incapacitated and there are no other fighters around to defend you, you need to know some basic self-defense."

"What?" The word came out as a whine and her shoulders dropped. She'd gotten excited at the idea of learning to fire a weapon, and now he was totally bursting her bubble. "C'mon. I'm not going to be carrying a set of car keys to stab a mugger."

"A woman your size can take down a man my size with little practice."

"Oh, balls," she muttered, and rolled her eyes. "You're really going to show me self-defense? How in the world do you expect me to be able to get close enough to jab my finger in an assailant's eyeball when he's carrying a machine gun? Or stomp on his foot when he's throwing a grenade at me?"

"Have you taken defense courses before?"

"Yeah, in college. Though a drunken frat boy isn't in the same realm as an Islamic extremist juiced up on jihad."

He mumbled something about her being impossible and a few other words she didn't quite catch. "Look, I'm trying to help you out here. Make you feel better about being outside the wire. Do you want my help or not? Because we can go back to the barracks and do a whole lotta nothing 'till morning."

She pressed her lips together, realizing this offer was more than she thought she'd get when she'd first asked. Besides, she knew she was too keyed up to sit in her room right now and focus on her story—or lack thereof. "Fine."

He clutched her wrist. "When someone grabs you by the arm—"

She brought her elbow in and twisted her arm, breaking his loose hold. "I know what an arm sweep is. Can't you do better than that?" She'd meant it more out of playful irritation. She had no doubt he could do much, much worse.

Without warning, he dropped his hand onto her shoulder, but Caitlin was ready. Her self-defense class might've been back in her college days, but after the uncomfortable encounter she'd had at the governor's mansion that night back in Arkansas, she'd brushed up and regularly practiced the skills she'd learned. She slammed her hand on top of his and swung her other arm around, knocking his away.

He didn't give her a break before his next attempt. He gripped her other shoulder harder than the last time, and she grabbed his hand again, this time capturing his thumb and twisting herself to make him bend over. Then she brought up her leg, but stopped short of actually kneeing him in the face, wanting to show him what she could do without actually hurting him. "Station also made us go through training before my first overseas assignment."

He shifted slightly and she grunted with effort to kept hold of him.

"Point taken. Now let go so I don't hurt you."

"You would expect me to let go of an attacker?" she teased.

She shouldn't have.

So fast that she wasn't able to process what had happened, he'd extracted himself, whirled behind her, and whipped his arm around her neck, slamming her back against his front.

She panicked and grabbed his arm, but he'd already gotten the upper hand.

"Should've tucked your chin."

Instead of responding, she wiggled, trying to get away. He was fast, but she'd practiced surprise attacks.

"Stop trying to wrestle me. You're just gonna waste energy."

Caitlin froze, knowing he was right.

"If you get pinned, your go-to move is to strike." He leaned in closer, his breath tickling her ear. "Stomp my foot. Dig those tiny little nails in my arm. Whatever you have to so you can turn. Then you can punch in the balls or hit the face."

She knew this. She should feel irritated with herself that she hadn't responded as quickly as earlier, but with him surrounding her, the only thing she could feel was heat. She was acutely aware of his arms around her, his mouth a hairsbreadth from her skin. Her heart took off even as she tried to keep from panting. She told herself to relax, ordered her body to release its tension, and somehow, she found the will to do so, to drop her hands from the arm currently caged around her neck. Unable to talk just yet, she nodded, and then eased her head against his chest.

Axle stiffened, and she realized when she'd thought she'd relaxed, she'd actually melted into him. Her back was one with his front, and when she'd dropped her hands, they weren't dangled beside her. She'd gripped the sides of his muscled legs. Why had she done that? Maybe she needed to help support herself, use him as an anchor to ground her. It didn't matter why she'd done it just that she had, and now she found it difficult to stop. He was hard, lean, hot. His heat completely engulfed her.

She shot a mental order to her hands to immediately let go of him, but she'd apparently lost all control over her body's actions. What was more shocking was why she didn't follow her internal command. It wasn't that she couldn't release him. She didn't *want* to. She liked the way he felt.

The hand he had on her belly eased, but he didn't take it away. His fingers spread ever so slowly, splaying across her tummy, his hot breath coming quicker, teasing her hair. The air suddenly became thinner when she realized his hand wasn't the only part of him she could feel moving. There was no space between them, so she knew the instant he got hard. She might have moaned at the feel of what this was doing to him. She didn't know. She had no idea what was happening, really. But she did make a sound, that she knew, because the moment it came from her lips, he cussed and released her.

Caitlin stumbled, no longer having him supporting her weight. But she stabilized herself quickly and faced him as her hormones rioted at the loss of contact.

He ran a hand though his hair. His muscles corded, lethal, deadly, she knew, but now another descriptor flew to the front of her head as his muscles rippled—*so incredibly sexy*.

"Sorry. That was out of line."

She continued her perusal of his body, admiring how strong and *male* he was. Her gaze lingered on the evidence of his arousal, missing the feel of it against her, and wondering how it would feel inside her.

He made a strangled sound. "Stop." Her gaze shot to him, and her cheeks warmed at being caught staring at his package.

Good grief, she needed to wrestle her hormones into submission. This wasn't her first day to ever be around an attractive man. *Hot.* She meant hot. She'd been around plenty of handsome men in her life. Hell, she'd been around plenty of sexy military men. This wasn't anything new. Yet, it was completely new. As often as she'd been around members of the opposite sex that oozed justifiable confidence, she'd never had to fight her body's reaction to a man before.

He swallowed. "That won't happen again," he said, obviously still trying to apologize.

Because she was both turned on by this man and shocked by her own body's reaction to him, she wanted to deny his words, yet agree and seek the privacy of her room to hide from him and whatever just happened...whatever *continued* to happen between them. She was so confused. By him. By herself.

Rather than go down a road that could totally embarrass her, she chose a route that would hopefully lighten the mood. With strength she did not feel, she smiled. "There are plenty of ways to distract an attacker." She shrugged.

He quirked an eyebrow and crossed his arms, though a smile played at his lips. "An effective technique."

"What can I say? My assets are limited. I can't be afraid to use any weapon in *my* arsenal."

He chuckled, but the heat was still in his eyes. "God help any man who tries to take you down."

"Maybe I was just looking for your gun."

"You know exactly where my gun is."

"What kind of lady would I be if I just reached for it?" She knew she was playing with fire with those words, but reason had checked out the moment she landed in this country.

"One who goes after what she wants," he said, seeing the fire she played with and stoking it more.

"True. But maybe I'll just wait for you to give it to me." She licked her dry lips. Neither one was talking about a firearm, and they both knew it. This man was dangerous.

More so than she could ever imagine, which was exactly why she needed to get this conversation back on track, no matter how much the thought of him giving her what she wanted lit her up. "Like your pen."

A slow smile spread across his face. "It is a tactical pen. You can take an eye out with it."

She rolled her eyes. "It amazes me you think it's more likely a man will sneak up behind me when *I* think the reality is one will shoot at me from across a field." Regardless of whatever was happening between the two of them, her situation in this war hadn't changed. There could be a chance she'd get stranded without protection. She'd slowly started to reason with herself that the chance was small, but it was there nonetheless.

He took a deep breath and dropped his arms as he regarded her. He glanced to the side, his gaze lingering out in the distance, and she got the feeling he was deciding something. The next words held no hint of the playfulness he'd just displayed. "I carry my assault rifle across my chest." He waved his hand in the area where she'd seen it on him before.

"I know."

Then he reached for the gun on his leg she'd spied earlier and pulled it out. "This is my sidearm." He holstered it. "I also have a knife here and here," he said, pointing to the one at his belt and one hidden on his ankle. "If something happens to me and my men, and you are in a life or death situation, Caitlin, life or death," he said again, slowly, pointing at her. "You can retrieve what you need off me to buy yourself time *until* you get rescued. If you need more ammo, here's where I'll have extra magazines."

She gaped at him, processing his words. It wasn't her own weapon like she'd wanted, but if she was completely honest, he gave her more of a concession than she should get. Her not having something like that on her person was a decision that came from up above. He really had no control over the matter.

A little bit of guilt ate at her. This man was willing to skirt the rules to make her feel better, so she should be completely honest with him...even if it meant he'd take the offer back. "I've never shot a gun."

"I'll show you how."

Her eyes popped, having not expected him to offer that, and a huge smile spread across her face. "Really?"

"This isn't playtime, Caitlin. These weapons are highly lethal."

Her hand snapped to her forehead. "Sir, yes, Sir." She echoed the line she'd heard from many of the people in uniform, knowing she didn't do it correctly, but too excited to care. Not only was he giving her access to his gear, he was going to show her how to use it all.

"Jesus. Stop doing that until I've had a chance to show you proper form."

She giggled, feeling lighter than she'd had all day. "Later. Right now, I get to handle your guns," she said quickly, a different kind of excitement now coursing through her veins. He was seriously going to let her practice with his guns!

"Don't think I'm going to just let you take my weapons either. I won't stop shooting until I'm dead. You got that? I'm serious. Life or fucking death, woman."

"Okay, okay." She couldn't control her stupid grin. "Life or death, yada, yada."

He groaned, but the miserable noise still sounded sexy coming from him. "C'mon, let's go do some shooting."

"Yay!" She jumped up and down, clapping, letting her excitement bubble over.

His eyes dropped to her chest, and she stilled, the heat from earlier only barely banked. He gritted his teeth and then jerked his head to the side, urging her to follow.

"Could definitely blow off some steam with some target practice," he muttered, though she didn't think he'd intended her to hear.

Whatever. Mr. Hot Badass Military Man was going to show her how to shoot. She briefly wondered if he was giving her permission to use his gun because he'd been caught up in the moment and knew he couldn't let her handle anything else that belonged to him. That thought did naughty things to her libido, but she tamped it down again.

He was a sexy man who was protecting her. Of course, she'd find him attractive—*handsome*. He was handsome only. To be attractive, there had to be more to him than anything purely physical. She'd remind herself of that as often as was necessary. He was yummy, all right, and any spark he ignited was understandable. But she couldn't afford to be attracted to him.

Not right now with how dangerous their surroundings were, and possibly not ever. Especially if Hunter told her things about him she loathed to hear.

CHAPTER SIX

AXLE HAD LOST count how many times he'd run around the barracks in the dark. He couldn't afford to workout away from Caitlin, but no way did he want to lose any sort of edge he had by not staying in optimal shape. Getting up extra early to exercise was his only option, and what he could do was limited to old-school methods. He ran laps, never venturing so far away that he lost sight of the building where she slept. He also did pushups, jumping jacks, burpees, and any other maneuvers that didn't require special equipment, only his body as the necessary resistance. He needed to keep his strength up, but that hadn't been his only motivating factor. He also had to do whatever he could to burn off the growing tension he'd been fighting.

When he couldn't lift weights, usually time at the shooting range was the next best thing to relieve any sort of pressure. Last night changed that. After their impromptu target practice, that source of stress relief had become tainted with heated memories.

Christ on a cracker, that woman was the wrong kind of deadly.

Oh, she hadn't been a natural. Her aim had been completely off initially. She'd been a quick study, though, after some personal critiques that were simple for her grasp, yet damn hard for him to get through. He'd had to stand from behind with his arms around her as he helped her sight in the target. It was something simple he'd done a hundred times before. It should've been clinical, not something erotic. Fuck, but it had been. It had been nothing short of torture. Several rounds of skin-on-skin contact torture. Her body was rounded and soft in all the right places. Luscious. Goddamn, she was beautiful. He'd been grateful he had to squat behind her to keep his head level with hers. Otherwise, she would've felt his raging hard-on pushed up against her. Not that it would've been the first time. He'd been sporting wood since their hot little exchange before they even got to the shooting practice part. It was why he knew going back to the range wouldn't do anything to help relieve tension.

So he ran, and ran, as if the hounds of hell nipped at his heels, stopping only to bang out enough pushups until his arms began to shake, and ran some more. By the time he was too exhausted to even think about her sexy body anymore, he decided to go a little more just to make sure. When he made it back to the barracks, his whole body was weak with spent energy and drenched with sweat. He had plenty of time to shower before she got up and rejuvenate himself with some coffee.

"Good morning, sir," Acker said when Axle walked through the main door. He'd been posted outside Caitlin's room when Axle left for his workout. He didn't see a need to keep someone there twenty-four-seven, but with Axle out of earshot, he wanted eyes on her door. "I see you enjoyed your scenic jog."

"What can I say? The tents are lovely this time of year." Axle quipped as he walked past. He didn't know Acker or the other men very well—not as well as his SEAL team—but there was a Naval bond already there. "Taking a shower."

"Good idea," he muttered.

Axle stopped and turned to look at him with the deadly glare time had perfected. Yes, there was a bond that might allow for some camaraderie, but he was still their team lead.

"I-I mean you want to stay ahead of trench foot. I hear that—"

"Enough, Acker," he said before continuing to the shower. "She get up early?"

"No, Sir. Not a peep."

"Good. At least I know she can follow directions when it comes to sleep." He knew jetlag was a bitch, so he tried to be mindful of that and let her have extra shuteye these first few mornings. "You can go get chow."

"Yes, Sir," he said with conviction, but without the volume to risk waking up Caitlin. It pleased him that this guy took that into consideration.

Axle had placed his towel and fatigues in the room before heading out on his run. Preparation was important, especially in a war zone. The last thing he wanted was a sudden new development that required immediate attention that he'd have to deal with wearing wet workout gear. Not that he expected shit to hit the fan before breakfast, but in a hot zone, one never knew.

He stripped and got under the cold water, hoping it'd cool the heat coursing through his body. It felt good, but after a couple of minutes, it hadn't started working. He grabbed the soap and started cleaning his body. It crossed his mind to take himself in hand and try relieving his stress another way, but he knew it wouldn't work. Oh, that would feel good, too, but any relief would only be temporary. If he started jacking off every time Caitlin filled his mind, he'd be damn raw. He couldn't afford to let thinking about her become an automatic erotic mental fantasy, which was exactly what would happen. That would be a dangerous path for many reasons, not the least bit being it clouding his judgment where she was concerned. He had a job to do, so the best thing for him was to ignore his physical reaction.

Cussing under this breath, he finished up his shower, dried off, and got dressed. He took his time, partly because she wouldn't be up for another fifteen minutes, but mainly due to his aching muscles slowing him down. Tiring himself before starting his day probably wasn't the best of ideas, but today they'd be doing flyovers. He wouldn't have to do a lot of walking around. Still, he probably should keep his work-outs shorter and find another way to relieve steam.

Not that, he scolded himself when his dick twitched, reminding him of a perfectly good option. He strapped on his gun and sheathed his knife more forceful than necessary.

Axle started down the short hall toward his room, but a sound coming from the other side of Caitlin's door drew his attention. He checked his watch. She still had another eight minutes before her alarm went off. Had she awoken early after all? Was she dreaming? He hesitated, watching, listening for any indication she was up already.

After about thirty seconds of silence, he turned toward his room. He was fucking hearing things now. He'd gone months before living in conditions that would test even the strongest of wills, but two damn days near this woman and he was losing his—

"No," she yelled, and Axle whipped around, bolting into her room. They were on base. She should be protected even when she was out of his sight, but in the seconds it took to bust through to her, a thousand different scenarios flashed in his mind.

All of them equally terrifying.

Yet none of them prepared him for what he saw.

———

CAITLIN'S ALARM went off right on schedule.

Her schedule.

She'd seen where Axle had listed on her itinerary when she was to arise, shower, and eat. She wasn't happy he'd planned everything out without discussing it with her first. It was the principle of the matter, regardless of how sexy he was. If she found it sweet of him to let her sleep in as long as possible, she quickly ignored that reaction. Yes, she was tired. And yep, she'd love nothing more than staying in bed and sleeping until dinnertime. She understood the need of him to book her time away from base. He wasn't only her guard, but her guide. She needed his help and had no problem cooperating with his timetable as it related to gathering information for her story. But it wasn't as if she didn't have any common sense. She was a grown woman and had worked in war zones before without every minute of her day being decided for her. Besides, there were two things he hadn't considered when taking it upon himself to make these decisions.

The first, and more important issue, was there was no time allotted for her to write. Her work wasn't just investigating the story and recording clips, but also writing reports for her producers and doing other necessary work behind the scenes. The boring paperwork stuff, the emails, and all the other minutia when creating a bombshell news piece were just as important as the video itself.

The second, and more pressing matter, pertained to needing time for her to make calls without him around. Granted, he wouldn't know the exact reason why she needed this time, but she was pretty sure military personnel reached out to people back home when they had the chance. He should've at least allowed her some privacy time to contact her family.

Hopefully, they'd get back earlier than noted on the printout she'd found in her room when she returned last night. That would give her some time to time to write up her notes and start crafting her story elements while the day's events were fresh on her mind. It would also give her an opportunity to jot down objectives for the next day. But that was later and not the reason she'd set her alarm thirty minutes earlier than scheduled.

And the clock was now ticking away at those few precious minutes she'd carved out for herself.

Without hesitation, she grabbed her laptop and opened the social profile she'd found and used to message Hunter. Nothing. Her shoulders slumped as she checked over it a second time. It looked more and more like this was a dummy account Maya had set up to tag her boyfriend, but upon closer inspection, the icon next to the message she'd typed to him had changed, signaling it had been read. Someone had seen her message. That didn't mean the person was Hunter.

Still slightly deflated, but not entirely surprised, she navigated to Heather's profile. Caitlin's heart raced when she saw Heather had responded, and she quickly clicked on the message.

Call me when you get up. I should be home from class by then.

Crap. She'd hoped for her brother's contact information since time was a premium, but she was grateful Heather had replied right away.

Caitlin clicked the video icon to initiate a call with her.

"Hey, girl!" Heather said from the other side.

Caitlin squinted from how bright the screen suddenly turned when the video connected. She had left her light off in her room, not wanting to alert any of the guys to her being awake. She threw the covers over her and her laptop.

"Are you making a blanket fort?" Heather asked.

Caitlin laughed slightly. "Not exactly." Though it totally looked like it. "Don't need to when I'm in a real one."

Heather nodded. "True, girl. And speaking of...how was your trip?"

"Long. Got in mid-day a couple of days ago and feels like I've been going non-stop ever since."

"They wasted no time, huh?"

"Nope. Got the tour, got the lecture, got tossed into the middle of fire. You're average war zone stuff."

Heather's mouth fell open. "Tell me you're kidding. Why does it look like you're not joking?"

"'Cause I'm not."

"What?" Heather whispered heatedly.

"Look, I'll give you the low down when I get back. We'll swap stories, catch up on everything, including any new developments with that guy Roc you told me about," Caitlin said, raising one eyebrow. She'd heard about how he'd come to her rescue, and from the sound of it, he'd had a crush on his coworker's sister. Heather bit her lip, and Caitlin smirked.

"There's nothing going on," Heather said quickly.

"Um-hmm, okay. Whatever. We'll talk all about your denial when I get back. Right now, I need some info from you not involving your love life. Or lack thereof."

"Is this your way of buttering me up? Because I gotta tell ya, you suck at it."

Caitlin chuckled. "Just keeping it real."

"All right, how can I help?"

"I need to find out about this guy who's showing me around—"

"Ohhh, what's that look?"

"What? I don't have a look."

"Call me, talking smack about a boy, all the while you got something going on with someone on the frontline." She shimmied in her seat like she was about to get the latest gossip.

"That's not why—"

"Don't you dare deny it. I've been around you too many times with my brother within a five-mile radius not to know what you look like when you're mooning over someone."

Did her cheeks get red? It felt like she was on fire. "It was a childhood crush," she defended. That lasted into young adulthood, but she wasn't going to admit that. "He's actually the reason I need to talk to you," she added slowly.

"Hunter?"

"Yeah. I need to know about the guy he arranged to protect me while I'm here. What's his story?"

Heather bit her lip, obviously fighting a smile. Her friend wasn't going to give up taunting her about him.

"I hate you," Caitlin muttered without any real anger.

"You love me...almost as much as you love solider boy."

"Jesus, can you focus for like three minutes? I don't have much time here."

"All right, all right." Heather waved her hand. "I don't

know anything about the guy really. Hunter said he called in a favor."

"Someone must've owed him big time if he was able to get a Navy SEAL to lead a team of men to be my personal bodyguards."

"What you do you mean a *team of men*? I thought he was going to get one guy to watch over you."

"If by *one*, you mean seven. And by *watch over*, you mean micromanage my every minute, then yes."

"Wow."

"Yeah. But I'm pretty sure it's the leader that got roped into doing this because of Hunter's involvement."

"Er, why? Couldn't it be any one of them?" she asked, furrowing her brow.

"Because he's the boss, and well, he made a comment when I met him that led me to believe this assignment isn't the norm."

"I doubt there's much normal about war."

"True, but I'd like to know how Hunter arranged this and just what he knows about the guy. Is he on this platform or have an active email address I can use to reach him?"

"Not really. I mean, he set up an account one day because Maya wanted him to RSVP for a party."

"Call Me Ishmael?"

Heather laughed. "Yep. She suggested Hermy the Frog, but he quickly rejected that. Still, he refused to put any personal information up there, and when she tagged him on a pic, he threatened to close the account if she did it again. Dude is seriously worried about having his information out there."

"Figured that was the case. I found that profile and tried messaging him, but wasn't sure if he ever really got on it."

"He probably checks it but is not active, if you know

what I mean. I'll tell him he needs to look for your message, though."

"Thanks. Not the first time I've come across a conspiracy theorist." In her line of work, she'd encountered a few sources who didn't want to be easily found, thinking the world was out to get them. "I really can't picture Hunter being the paranoid type."

"He's not. There's a lot you don't know about him," she said, frowning slightly.

"So I've heard. Care to tell me now?" When Heather had said this before, Caitlin was heading out of the country. Plus, they hadn't actually been away from prying ears to talk freely.

Heather glanced to the side. "Okay, look, he got into some real shit back in Dallas after he moved away."

"Like, what kind of trouble are we talking about here?"

"The mafia kind."

"What?" Caitlin asked, drawing out the one-word question.

"He's not proud of it, and he got out before things got really bad," she added quickly. "Remember Maya's ex?"

"How can I forget? Dude kidnapped you." Not that she'd ever met the guy, but she'd heard all about him after Maya came into the picture.

"Right, and there's a connection with all that to Hunter's past, but that's not really the point here."

"I'm not following." Heather was speaking in circles.

"Long story short, Hunter's bad boy past is how he became involved with The Bang Shift."

"Why does a garage care about his past as long as he can do the work?" Unless she meant they hadn't held his questionable youth against him when hiring him. Caitlin got the feeling it wasn't that simple.

"Because they're all not *just* mechanics."

"What does that mean?" She gasped. "Is it a chop shop? Do they steal cars and sell them?"

"No, not that, but remember that guy who owned the garage before?"

She knit her brow, scanning her memory. "Um, Sheppard, something."

"Yeah. He brought all of those guys together to work on cars *legitimately*, but they're mainly mercenaries. They work on cars as more of a side gig."

Her words slowly clicked into place. Mercenaries? How was that even possible? It was such a small place, away from large cities and borders. It was a peaceful town. She admittedly fell out of the loop on what was going on in Mayflower, Arkansas the last couple of years while she worked night and day in Atlanta on her career, but surely she'd have heard about this.

Unless they were so good they'd managed to keep it secret all these years. That didn't seem possible. Her job had shown her there was always a weak link willing to sell a story.

She quickly thought back to what she did know to figure out why she'd missed this. She knew Bear bought the garage after the previous owner had died in an accident. *Oh no.* Had they killed him? That's what mercenaries did. They killed people.

For money.

She hadn't had any dealings with those who engaged in that sort of thing, but she'd covered a story once on mercenaries kidnapping a humanitarian. It hadn't been about murder then, but the motivation had still been the same.

Money. That she did know. Everything they did was about the almighty dollar.

Was Axle somehow involved? He'd said he'd rather be taking out marks than protecting her. Did that mean he was a mercenary, too? Was he doing this for money? Had he been *hired* to watch her, rather than just *assigned* to protect her? She'd assumed Hunter had pulled strings to make it happen, not open a wallet.

A more alarming thought hit her. Had Axle killed people for money? "No," she yelled, yanking the covers off, needing to break free of physical and mental blocks she'd had in place. No way. No. Way! That couldn't be. None of this could be true.

"Whatever you're thinking, girl, I don't think it's *that* bad—"

Her door busted open, banging on the opposite wall, and Axle stormed in.

She squeaked, slamming her laptop shut on instinct that had been propped on her lap, and gaped at him. "What the hell?"

His wild gaze darted around the room, looking for something. The other guys shuffled in behind him, all cramped in her room. Just barged in without any warning.

How dare he come in here like this.

"Are you kidding me?" she yelled, tossing her computer to a pillow and jumping up from the bed. She was not through talking to Heather, but she didn't want Axle knowing she was digging into him. "Just what do you think you're—"

"Why did you scream?" he demanded.

"None of your business. I didn't scream for you," she said, crossing her arms. Her mind was still reeling at the possibility this man wasn't just a warrior for the government, but one for the private sector too. She glared at him. "You'd know it if that happened."

She was baiting him, and she didn't care. As he took in the room and the men behind him, his stance began to relax. Whatever had instigated this, he'd obviously jumped to the wrong conclusion.

"What's going on? What did I miss?" Acker asked, mouth around a muffin as he strolled into the room. She hadn't realized he'd been missing a few seconds ago. Although he'd asked it casually, his other hand reached for his sidearm. She instinctively raised her arms.

Oh, crap. Where all these guys mercenaries? She had no idea just how far this secret element even went, but she had to act normal until she figured it out. They'd think something was off if she didn't stand up to them. She'd already shown them she had a feisty streak.

"Your fearless leader, that's what." She turned to Axle, staring daggers. He ran his hand through his hair.

"I can see you're mad—"

"I'm *pissed.*" That was true, but it was just one facet of the myriad of emotions coursing through her. She had so much to process. "Get out."

"Yes, ma'am," one of the guys said, which looked to irritate Axle all over again.

"Don't move," he ordered but never took his gaze off her. "Like I said. I can see you're mad, and I apologize for coming in—"

"Barging. For barging in." She dropped her arms and put her hands on her hips. "You interrupted an important call."

"You did not have anything on your schedule. Had I known you had a meeting, this could have been avoided."

"Unlike those guys," she said, pointing at each man crowding around him, "I don't take orders from you."

"While you're here, you do."

"Get bent, asshole." A risky move calling him a name, she knew that, but anger and confusion were beating out shock and fear at the moment. If Hunter was paying this guy, that changed everything. She respected men in uniform. Really, she did, but if he was being compensated for this, she sure as hell wasn't going to blindly fall in line with whatever he said.

Not that she'd been eager about it before.

His face turned red, and the men behind him took a few steps back. Caitlin immediately regretted letting her rage get the best of her. If he was a mercenary who killed for money, maybe he would also eliminate someone he considered a nuisance.

A mouthy one at that.

God, she hoped this man wasn't a contract killer.

Get it together. She swallowed in an effort to bring some moisture back into her suddenly dry throat. Although the thought of him being a cold-blooded murderer had just taunted her, she had no proof of that.

Nor did she want to truly believe it.

Her conversation with Heather had just gotten her mind soaring with all kinds of scenarios, and she needed time to wrap her head around it all to be able to look at this news objectively. Hunter was a mercenary. That she did know. She just wasn't sure of anything else at this point.

Axle checked his watch, and then slowly said, "You have thirty-seven minutes before we have to be at the helicopter."

He didn't wait for her to respond. He turned around, barked at the men to meet him outside, and closed the door behind him.

Without hesitation, she dove for the bed and opened

her laptop. She tried to call Heather back, but she didn't answer. She opened a message to Hunter.

Talked to Heather, and she confirmed this is your account. We need to talk. I'll have an Internet connection again in fourteen hours or so. I'll try to reach you then.

The bombing wouldn't be the only big story she had to work on while in this battleground, but where her official assignment would be easy to remain objective, she knew this other one would be much more difficult to draw that line

Her old crush was a mercenary, and this new guy could be one too.

Didn't matter how hot he was. If he was hired gun, she'd ignore any more attraction to him—yes, attraction. She had to admit that to herself. It was why she'd been more shocked of the possibility of Axle being a mercenary than by the news of Hunter actually living that life.

If Axle was one, she'd make sure she didn't grow anymore attached to him, and the only way she knew how to stop it in its tracks was getting him and his team off this assignment.

Because if he was working her, any interest he'd shown might not have been genuine.

He could be playing her...completely.

CHAPTER SEVEN

Axle stormed out of the barracks with his team falling in line behind him. The blood rushed in his veins and heart pounded with effort that shouldn't even be there, but he was angry, and worse, he couldn't do anything about it.

Caitlin was right. He'd barged in unannounced. Yes, she'd screamed, and yes, he had every right to make sure she was okay, but he was letting her get to him on a mental level, and it was really screwing up his game.

He took two deep breaths before facing his men. "What is the status of the helo?"

"Preflight checklist is being conducted, sir," Glick said. The man was one of the quieter ones on the team, but seemed to be the most laser focused.

"I don't want a repeat of yesterday."

"No, Sir," they all said.

He relaxed his stance a little, getting into the right headspace for this assignment. "I know we can't predict when insurgents will strike, but we can do better." He looked at each of the men. "I need a drone. Anyone have an Air Force connection with a qualified pilot?" If they didn't, that was fine. Part of being on a team not only involved utilizing those members' skills, but also their knowledge. Once the Major General approved the use an unmanned aerial vehicle for reconnaissance, the man would ensure he was assigned a member with the appropriate credentials. However, Axle always preferred to use people who'd proven their abilities in the real world, not just good marks on simulations for certification purposes.

He got several negative responses and a couple of names, but those two were either stationed in another country or home from deployment. He sent Glick to inquire with the pilot assigned to their flyovers for recommendations.

Axle went over the stops on today's schedule with the remaining members to make sure they all understood what was expected. He then executed several orders to the others in preparation for today's mission. Once he dismissed them to conduct their assignments, he turned back to the barracks.

And stopped.

He was close enough to keep an eye on the building from here without invading her personal space again. He wanted to go back in, though, which was even more reason not to.

Pinching the bridge of his nose, he pulled out his phone.

"Major General Burge," his new commander answered.

"Sorry to bother you so early, Sir."

"The war never sleeps."

"Yes, Sir," he said. "You are aware of the complication we endured yesterday." It wasn't a question. Axle was aware the man stayed up to speed on everything that happened to the men and women of this base and especially when they traveled off it.

He cleared his throat. "It's dangerous out there. That's why I have you protecting her, Landry."

"Understood. I'd like UAV use permission, Sir."

"For how long?"

"Every day."

"Do you have any idea how much that'd cost?"

"Yes, Sir, which is why I wouldn't request it unless I felt it was necessary. Satellite surveillance isn't enough."

He didn't say anything right away. "Has anyone ever saved your life, Landry?" he asked as if contemplating something greater than what they'd just been discussing.

"Yes, Sir. Had my sights on a target for about five hours outside a known killing field, waiting for a clean shot that wouldn't give up my location. We'd been keeping watch of a small stealth group of insurgents who'd been making their way toward us." He hesitated. "But they had a member who'd broken off from the group long before we saw them. He came in from the opposite direction."

"So they found you before you found them," he said matter-of-factly.

"Yes, Sir. My spotter saw him a split second before I did. He threw his knife, lodging it in the shooter's throat right before his gun discharged. The bullet ricocheted three inches from my head."

"And did that make you feel like you owed the spotter one after that? That if he asked you to do something, you'd do it for him no questions asked?"

"Yes, Sir, but he's my brother. I'd do anything for any one of them." Even the ones who hadn't saved his life directly because they all had done so one way or another year after year. It was what made teamwork so vital in special operations. If someone failed in their role, it could cause a catastrophic domino effect. They all needed and counted on each other. "Of course, he likes to remind me of the time he saved my ass whenever he gets a chance, Sir."

He chuckled, but then went silent again. "What if he hadn't survived? What if, instead of living, he gave his life for yours? How would you repay that kind of debt, Commander?"

"That kind can never be repaid, Sir, but I would make it my life's mission to try anyway."

"You're a good warrior, Landry. We need more like you in all branches of military."

"Thank you, Sir." That meant a lot coming from someone as decorated as the Major General. Not that it explained why their conversation detoured down this path.

The man paused, and Axle could sense a shift in his demeanor before he said anything else. These questions had been poignant, he knew that. The Major General was a smart and methodical man. He could assess a situation and contemplate all possible scenarios before asking one question. "UAV will track your flight plan and return to base for regular assignment. It won't be with you throughout the day, but it'll at least ensure your path is initially clear of combatants."

"Thank you." It wasn't as good of an option as tracing their routes throughout the day, but it was a step in the right direction that would help protect them in the field.

"And Landry, the faster Cooper finishes her investigation into the MOAB, the quicker we can get back to normal."

"I like normal, Sir."

"Me, too. Although, you are right. Repaying a life debt

is a never-ending responsibility." With that, he disconnected the call.

Axle had no idea who had saved the Major General's life, but he had no doubt something awful happened in his past that would forever bind him to that man's legacy.

A legacy that was somehow attached to Caitlin Cooper.

CHAPTER EIGHT

AFTER TWO DAYS OF FLYOVERS, Caitlin was finally allowed on the ground to talk with locals. That hadn't been the original plan, but Axle had said something about a drone intercepting fire and having to modify the schedule. If it didn't delay her investigation, she'd find it funny that his precious agenda got all jacked up. Once they were back from surveying the land, she attempted to question people on the base about the bombing, but that had gotten her nowhere.

Her official assignment hadn't been the only story that had stalled. She hadn't been able to reach Hunter either. She tried contacting him that evening as she'd told him, but he hadn't picked up. Not only that, but there'd been no reply from him. She messaged him morning and night the last couple of days after each attempt at contacting him through the chat feature on the social media platform. After no luck again this morning, she fired off a lengthy message to Heather about needing her help reaching him.

Then she went to Maya's profile and messaged her about reaching him. If he wouldn't listen to his sister, maybe he'd listen to his girlfriend. She'd try reaching him again when she got back to base this evening.

Now, she was in Nangarhar, interviewing several of the local tribe members. It hadn't been easy winning their trust. She was an American on their land. Just because they appreciated the fight against the Taliban and ISIS didn't mean they welcomed outsiders with open arms. The bomb dropping nearby certainly hadn't helped smooth their ruffled feathers. Each time she asked someone new about it, Asad had to rush to translate the frustrations echoed from all.

It had taken a while, but eventually, she'd gotten into her stride. With each new person she met, she'd been directed to another with just a little bit more information than the last. Lorenzo was a genius behind the camera, making sure to capture all the best angles during the interviews, and when she'd been hunting down each new lead, he also filmed various groups of people going along their normal lives. When someone refused to talk on camera, he focused on Caitlin as she took notes...with the cool pen Axle had let her use. She should probably give it back to him before she lost it. She had a feeling it'd be a lot cheaper to buy a bag of Bics than risk misplacing his special one. She like using it, though. It was very fluid, and it was his. She quickly pushed that thought away and focused on her work.

All the material Lorenzo captured would be useful to them. Most would be spliced in with the interviews she conducted to tell the complete story. The rest could be used for teasers or intros for smaller online news segments. She could already tell this was going to be an amazing piece for the network.

If she could find the compelling hook her producer knew was out there.

The last young man she'd spoken with told her of his uncle, saying the man had been out with his goats when he saw suspicious men. Caitlin followed the young guy to his uncle and asked him some questions. The uncle confirmed he'd seen those suspicious men his nephew first discussed, but said his wife had talked directly to one of them. When she learned this, she had to contain her excitement. This could be the break she was hoping for! She asked to speak to her, but the man refused to allow his wife to come out of their home.

Not with foreign military men in the village.

She understood. Besides the typical weariness she encountered, there was additional concern palpable in the air. Axle and some of his team were visible to everyone, so there was no denying it added to the tension of the small crowd. For all they knew, his men could be part of the group who bombed the area. Their presence definitely made her job harder.

Okay, technically, she wouldn't even be able to out here if it wasn't for them, but whatever.

Working with the interpreter, she'd cajoled the villager into letting her speak to the older woman. When he agreed, it was for Caitlin to go to her, and not the other way around. She had no choice but to agree.

The uncle led Caitlin, Lorenzo, and Asad into their home to talk to his wife. When she got in, she woman was visibly shaken. She introduced herself calmly and tried not to seem too intimidating.

"Ask her where she was when she saw the men," she said to Asad. He repeated her question in *Pashto*.

The woman glanced to her husband. He motioned his approval, and she replied.

Asad translated, "In the field near the goats."

Good. "And how many men did you see?"

"Nine."

"Your husband said you spoke to one. Is that correct?" she asked softly, hoping the lady be able to understand her demeanor even though the words wouldn't be immediately clear.

"Yes." She nodded again as Asad translated.

"What did he say to you?"

Suddenly, the woman became animated, saying what seemed like quite a lot. Caitlin could feel the excitement and glanced at Asad several times, but he kept his focus on the local until she finished speaking.

She paused, and Asad turned to Caitlin. "He said to go back to the village and not come out until morning. It wasn't safe to meet *mother*." Asad used air quotes on the last word. The woman had a confused expression on her face, but Caitlin understood the message loud and clear.

"How many days was this before the air strike?"

"Two. Yes, two days."

"Did he say anything else?"

The woman nodded before she spoke, but before Asad translated, he asked her something. They talked back and forth before Asad focused on Caitlin. "He asked her if she'd seen anybody selling military weapons."

"What?" Caitlin asked, rearing back. What did that have to do with anything? "Did she?"

"No. She just told me that one of the village men had been recruited into ISIS, and he'd come back the week before the bombing. There was talk that he'd negotiated a deal with Americans for weapons."

Her mouth fell open. "An American selling weapons to ISIS?"

Asad's head bobbed side-to-side. "An American military man."

What the... "Who was the buyer? The guy from the village, I mean."

Asad began to translate her question, but a loud noise cut him off. Caitlin jumped at the sudden sound, and the other woman shrieked in fear.

"Caitlin," Axle shouted from the front of the house. Relief flooded her it was only him. She turned to face his direction, ready to explain what she was doing, but before she could step out of what she likened to a den, he was right there. "What the *hell* are you doing?"

She pointed to the older lady, who was scrambling to stand behind her husband. "This woman spoke to someone in the military before the bombing." Caitlin stopped short of the weapons details. She needed to get more information before she let that knowledge out. If someone in the military was actually selling arms to ISIS, that was huge.

It wasn't just intel on the bombing. It was a scoop. Something bigger than she'd even dreamed.

Axle's gaze shot to the woman. His eyes narrowed a bit before looking down to Caitlin. "I don't give a fuck," he said flatly. "You are *not* to leave my sight."

"Sorry, but she wasn't allowed to leave the house to speak to me. I had no choice."

"I've been here the whole time," Lorenzo said. Axle's head whipped in his direction where he stood in the back of the room with his camera aimed at her and the locals.

"Stick to shooting video. Let me worry about the big boy stuff."

Crap. Caitlin grabbed his shirt. "Hey. You don't have to be rude, and you're freaking them out," she whispered heatedly. He grabbed her wrist and yanked it off him.

"Wrap it up. We're done for the day."

"But we've only been here a few hours." She had to strike while the iron was hot! Once she left, they might not be willing to talk to her again.

"Done," he repeated, and backed away. He crossed his stupid arms over his stupid chest and glared at her. She'd not known him long, but she knew him well enough not to hope he'd change his mind.

Caitlin shuffled over to Asad. "Tell them we have to leave, but we'll be back tomorrow—"

"Nope," Axle said, cutting in. "We're dropping to another quadrant tomorrow. And we're sure as shit not disclosing where ahead of time." He looked at her like she'd lost her mind.

"Right," she muttered, and looked at Asad. That made sense, not that she liked it. "Thank her for her time and let her know if I get a chance to come back and ask more questions, I'll bring some fruit as an offering."

Because she would be back. She didn't know how she'd swing it, but this woman could be the only firsthand witness to the bigger arms story. No way was she leaving this conversation at that.

Once Asad finished relating her information, she smiled and nodded her goodbye before following Axle out of the house.

With each step farther and farther away, Caitlin got madder at him for shutting down her interview. He had no idea how hard it was getting people to talk...and that didn't include the repressed class of women in this country. The fact that her husband had agreed to the interview and the lady actual told her some interesting information were both more than she expected to get this soon into her investigation. Especially after getting zilch from questioning the troops.

She wanted to bite his head off, but he was busy barking orders in his mouthpiece and listening with his ear thingy as he walked beside her toward the helicopter. As they got closer, the other men traveling with her materialized from various directions and converged around her. Once they all loaded in the aircraft, Axle reached for Caitlin's the harness.

"I got it!" she yelled over the whirl of the propeller and grabbed for it instead. She did not need his help with *anything*.

He gently knocked her hands away and fastened her in before strapping into the seat beside her.

Within moments, they were airborne, and Caitlin's anger soared with them. She kept her gaze locked away from the brute sitting beside her and stewed.

She had no problem with him protecting her, but she hadn't been in any danger when he'd ordered their evacuation from the village. Caitlin knew how to follow rules. Heck, she understood why there were rules in the first place, but what he did was flex his authority muscle. Nothing else.

The return trip took as long as it had to get to Nangarhar this morning, but it felt like it only took minutes. When they landed, she ripped at her harness, and stomped off the aircraft before he could have a chance to free her.

"Caitlin," he called after her.

She didn't turn around. She knew they were going to load up into the same ATVs they'd arrived in that were parked nearby. He must've gotten the hint because he didn't say anything else; rather, he let her storm off.

She climbed into the same seat she'd occupied that

morning. Axle and others got in. She wasn't sure who else rode with them this time, and she didn't care to look. They'd jumbled around each time they'd gotten into a vehicle, but Axle was always with her.

Always. And when he wasn't with her, it was always on his terms. Not hers. It was never Caitlin's decision to be out of his eyesight. He demanded control.

Yeah, he was definitely the link to Hunter. He was too involved and too much like the bossy man she grew up with not to be the one he put on her.

Heather had commented that it could've been one of the other guys, but there was no way that was true. Axle was too invested in her protection—in her—not to be the one who had the most at stake here.

When they pulled up to the barracks, she hopped out, but her anger was a living thing. Before she thought better of it, she turned around and faced him. "I hope they sure as hell are paying you enough money to screw me over."

He reared back as if she'd slapped him, but his expression quickly blanked before morphing into one of incredulity. "Nowhere near enough, baby. That's for goddamn sure."

Someone behind him snickered, and his face turned to stone. It was a look she was sure would instill fear in whoever caused it, but he didn't look away from her. No doubt he would deal with the guy later once he was through putting up with Caitlin and her mouth. He wouldn't have to wait long.

"I'm going to my room to make some calls to keep working on the story you just ripped me away from. I know it's hard for you, but I'd really appreciate it if you didn't come barging in."

She didn't wait for a response. She was up the stairs before he replied, "You have until chow time."

"Sir, yes, Sir!" she said mockingly before walking in and slamming the door.

She heard his barking commands from outside. She would've winced at how pissed he sounded if she wasn't knee deep fury in it herself. She tossed her stuff down onto her bed and whipped the hijab off her head with an angry huff. She held in the scream that lodged in her throat. If she let it free, that...that...that *jerk* would come barging in.

She'd found him damn near irresistible before, and now she wanted to knee him in the balls like she'd learned how to do back in college.

"That sorry son of a bitch," she muttered, stalking around her tiny room. She unlaced her shoes and kicked them off, a low growl escaping as the second one flew across the room and landed against the wall. She pulled her shirt off, leaving the tank on. It was hot, and dirty, and dry, and all of that miserableness just compounded her anger. If she could pummel him, she would. She should so march right back outside and go toe-to-toe with him. But the man was like a million times stronger than she was. She wasn't an idiot, nor was she one to condone unnecessary violence. But the thought of inflicting pain eased a little of her fury.

Just a little.

It took several breaths before she could turn to her notebook and begin scanning the information jotted down earlier. She groaned at how little there was as she dropped to the bed, but as soon as she landed, she yelped and shot up. Something stabbed into her leg. She looked at the blanket, fearing some desert-dwelling insect had stung her, and knowing if she had to go ask Axle for medical attention, she'd stay here and die a slow miserable death instead.

But it was much worse than some creepy crawly. That red haze from before? Oh, it was back as she stared down at Axle's fancy shamancy tactical pen. He hadn't asked for it back, and since she knew it could be used as a weapon, she hadn't felt inclined to return it. She cursed it and him to the pits of hell and flung it across the room.

She needed to call her boss, but she was too frustrated to talk about work. Besides, it was about midnight back home. Too late for a meeting. She sent him an email instead, detailing what happened today and what information she'd come across. Crafting that correspondence helped her focus more on work and less on the warrior probably standing guard outside. Yes, this was exactly what she needed to be doing. After dinner, she would get with Lorenzo and start going over the footage they gathered. She'd have more for her segment tomorrow, hopefully some smaller pieces they could air whenever they wanted with some teaser shots for what was to come.

Once that was done, she pulled up her notes on the men she attempted to question on base, trying to find any connection between military personnel and who might've been in the village before the bombing. As she clicked through the pages, she kept glancing at the clock. It might've been too late to contact her boss, but the same rules of etiquette didn't necessarily apply to friends.

Switching gears, she opened the social media platform she'd used to contact Hunter and Heather. Heather had messaged, but it was only chitchat. Caitlin responded in kind.

There was nothing from Hunter.

Still.

She spied the call icon and hesitated. It *would* be pretty late in Arkansas, but Hunter always was a night owl.

Besides, she'd gone the asking-permission route and it hadn't gotten her anywhere. Calling this late would fall into the asking-for-forgiveness side, but she was running out of options. She clicked on the call feature with the messaging app on Hunter's profile.

It rang and rang. She was about to hang up when it connected.

"You're a pain in the ass," Hunter said.

Caitlin gasped when she heard him speak, excited to finally reach him. "You mean *determined*."

"Nope. Pretty damn sure getting me in trouble with my girlfriend makes you a pain in the ass."

If Maya was the only one that convinced him to talk to her, she owed her big time. "Well, I'm not the one avoiding calls. What does that make you?"

"Busy. Not avoiding you, darlin'. Just been swamped."

That statement held much more meaning then it did before. "Are you talking about cars or contracts because I've learned there's more to your little shop than sparkplugs."

He grunted. "Heather has a big mouth."

"This is not news."

He chuckled. "Yeah, and neither is my life," he said with a little humor, but with a finality that couldn't be missed. His life would not be an open book to her, no matter who she was friends with. "You got questions for me. That shit better be off the record. You understand?"

She hated those words. Normally, she'd do her best to get them taken off the negotiating table, but he had personal information she needed. This wasn't for her assignment, so she reluctantly agreed. "Fine. How do you know this guy?"

"What guy?"

She sighed. "Don't play dumb."

She heard someone mumble in the background, and he

said, muffled, "Maya, I'm not being difficult. Fuck." She obviously wasn't happy he wasn't being very forthcoming with Caitlin, and for that she was grateful. Maya had definitely earned some major girl points. Hunter muttered something else under his breath that sounded like he was cursing all women to the depths of hell before he said a little clearer, "I don't know him."

"What does that mean?" How in the world did he not know the guy he arranged to protect her?

"Just what I said. I know powerful people. Those people arranged it for me."

That crashing sound was all of her hopes crumbling around her. "So you can't tell me anything about him? What he does in the military? If he's even in the military? If he's a mercenary like you? If he's even married?"

She'd been sure Hunter was the key to unlocking the mystery of Axle, but she'd been trying to open the wrong door all along.

He snickered. "Married? Why do you care if he's married?"

"Because she likes him," Maya called out.

Well, that woman just lost half of her points.

"Oh," Hunter said, all serious again.

"I'm an inquisitive person. Nothing wrong with that," she defended. "Plus, he's around all the time and is in charge of my security. I have a right to know if he's on the level."

"So this is for your personal information?"

"Yes. I already agreed it was off the record."

"Fine. I still don't know him—"

"Hunter," she said, cutting him off.

"But, he's not a mercenary." He chuckled. "Not a fan of

that word, by the way. Most of our work has been contracted by the federal government."

"Oh," she said, genuinely surprised. If the feds used them, then maybe they weren't the stereotypical crime syndicate she'd imagined. Unless, the jobs they did for the government were seedy assignments the feds wanted done under the radar. *"Oh."*

"Caitlin," he said, warning.

"Are you telling me the federal government pays you to commit crimes?"

"You know I'm not answering that, even though this conversation is off the record," he said, stressing those three little, ugly words.

"Right. You're right. I'm sorry." There was a whole lot he wasn't telling her, and from the sound of how deep the story went, she couldn't blame him. She had enough things to focus on right now.

Doesn't mean I can't get more info out of him and his garage buddies once I'm back in the States. There was a story there, but those guys would have to agree to her prying into their business in order to make it happen. She doubted they'd let her do that.

Wouldn't stop her from trying, though. Later.

"As far as I know, he's not married," Hunter said. He probably knew that topic would jolt her out of her thoughts on the Bang Shift Garage.

"Good."

Hunter chuckled. "Maya was right."

"I'm always right," she yelled.

Caitlin wasn't going to justify that with a response. "What else?" she asked instead.

"Nothing. Like I said, I've never met him. The feds arranged it."

"Wow, the government must really want to keep you guys happy if they're willing to give you whatever you want when you snap your fingers."

"That's far from true, but these are feds I know. Very well."

"Who are they?"

"Nope."

"Hunter."

"No way. Who they are is none of your business. I've answered your questions. The guy watching you is legit. He really is in the military. A Navy SEAL, I'm told. He's not a mercenary...at least not on my team." He'd rattled off answers to the questions she'd initially asked. "Can't really say if he's married, but if you want, I can find out at lunch and pass you a note in study hall."

"Funny. But I had more questions than that."

"Don't think there's much else I can tell you."

She sighed, but at least some of her fears were alleviated. Axle hadn't been hired to protect her. He hadn't assumed a role of a military operative. He really was one.

He hadn't lied to her.

"He's bossy," she muttered, and once she confessed that, more rolled from her mouth. "He barks orders and insists on doing things his way. He got all mad when I went into a village today to question locals. The whole place was surrounded. I was only out of his view for like three minutes, and he pulled me out of there, stopping what was probably a major break in my story."

"You need to listen to him," Hunter said, brooking no argument. "He's there to protect you. You shouldn't make it difficult for him."

"He shouldn't stop me from doing my job."

Hunter hesitated, then said, "Sounds like to me y'all need to communicate."

"He's around me every waking minute." The last thing she needed was more time with him. He incited something within her. Anger. Passion.

Emotion.

She didn't know how to deal with that.

"Yet, you call me late at night, halfway around the world, to ask if he's married when you could've asked him yourself?"

"It's not that simple."

He laughed. "Women. Always making everything so damn complicated."

"Yeah, yeah. Point taken." Realizing she'd gotten everything she was going to from Hunter, she wrapped up their conversation and ended the call. She was still mad at Axle, but maybe Hunter was right.

She needed to reason with Axle, make him understand how important her work was so he could help, not hinder, her progress. She didn't expect him to go out of his way to get the answers she needed, but it'd be nice if he wouldn't work against her either.

Sounded good in theory, but it was going to be easier said than done.

CHAPTER NINE

THIS WOMAN WAS GOING to be the death of him.

After the close call they'd experienced the first day out, Axle had been relieved the following days' flyovers had gone off without a hitch. Although sitting next to her in a helo most of those days had put him on another kind of edge. Her knee would brush his accidentally, and his cock would twitch, not caring she hadn't meant anything by it. And then there'd been the times she touched him on purpose to get his attention and point to something. He'd had to force himself to follow her direction and not gape at where her hand was on his arm, shoulder, hand, leg. Once she even reached over and touched him without looking at him, and she'd grazed dangerously close to his groin area. No amount of mental explanation could stop his cock from stirring.

Yep, she was killing him. One nonchalant touch at a time. Even though the light touches had been damn near maddening, it'd been a break from the intensity of their shooting practice. The time in the helo had helped him focus on Burge's revelation and pushed him to regain his focus. She was a job, and he had a responsibility to ensure her safety.

Nothing else.

The faster, the better.

Especially since she didn't seem to understand how important it was for her to follow orders all the time. No matter what. He had no idea how she ranked his instructions, but it was always a crapshoot with her whether or not she would fucking listen to him. Like yesterday in Nangarhar, Axle had watched her from several feet back while she'd interviewed locals for several hours. There'd been a couple of young Afghan men who'd gotten a little too close for his comfort, and he'd quickly put himself between Caitlin and the tribe members. She'd been quick to follow his command then. He knew jumping in caused some of the people surrounding her to be apprehensive, but he didn't care. It was her safety that mattered. Regardless, she'd managed to ease the tension with those she'd been talking to and had quickly gotten back into her groove. Things had been smooth again...until she'd decided upon herself to go into one of the huts without okaying it with him first.

Because he sure as shit wouldn't have allowed it.

And she goddamn knew it.

Pushing aside his irritation from yesterday, he watched her for a few more seconds, trying not to glare at her and probably not succeeding very well, before focusing on the interpreter. Axle wasn't familiar with him, but Lorenzo had worked with the Afghan man a few months ago on some other assignment and had vouched for him.

Not that Lorenzo's word meant anything. The few times Axle had been around him, he got a weird vibe from the dude. He was aware he had no grasp on journalism, nor did he have the desire to figure it all out, but it seemed the videographer liked doing things his way. Shouldn't Caitlin have some control over how the news piece was recorded? The man tended to lead Caitlin in his direction, rather than accepting her input and letting her report how she wanted. Axle didn't have to understand filming the news to know he didn't like that. This was her gig, though, so he let that part slide.

Lorenzo's pushiness didn't stop there. When the cameraman wasn't focused on controlling their work, Lorenzo flirted with Caitlin. It didn't take a rocket scientist to see that. She'd chatted and laughed with him while they'd been working together these last few days, but she'd also kept a little distance between them, only getting close enough to review some footage. Still. Seeing him make pass after pass at her? Yeah, that pissed Axle off. He had no right to be mad, but it left a bad taste in his mouth nonetheless. And if it made him not like the guy even more, he didn't give a fuck. He didn't have to be buddies with Lorenzo to protect Caitlin.

He knew the basics about Lorenzo, but he didn't trust him or his word. Just because he'd said the interpreter was stellar didn't matter. He'd had Asad checked out before letting him near Caitlin.

Pulling his gaze away from Lorenzo and Asad, Axle took out his binoculars and scanned the area. His guys had set up a perimeter and checked in on schedule, but Axle preferred to doublecheck. He hated surprises, especially the dangerous kind. It was better to be prepared than caught unawares. Every fifteen minutes, he personally scanned the border of the village, looking for any threats. It only took a few seconds, but it was worth it for his own peace of mind.

When he finished his sweep, he turned to where Caitlin had been standing with the guys working with her.

"Shit," he breathed. Ice shot down his back. She wasn't standing there anymore. "Not again."

Without hesitation, he moved to where he'd last seen her, eyes scanning the thin crowd. Like yesterday, they were in a small village, mud houses surrounded them, and the locals moved about, probably curious about the newcomers and their helicopter. There was no sign of her.

He tapped his comm. "Bravo Team One, no eyes on Charlie, come in." Caitlin's codename was Charlie. He'd chosen it since it was the military phonic for the letter C. He wanted to keep her actual name out of radio communications, and it was short for Charlie Foxtrot. *Clusterfuck.*

"This is Bravo Team one. Charlie and Lightweight are beside the house on your two. Over."

"Copy," Axle said as he headed toward the house just to his right. *Lightweight* wasn't phonic for shit. But he figured he'd stick to utilizing the first-letter-of-the-first-name method, and it was a better option than *Loser* for Lorenzo.

Axle rounded the corner at a dead speed, not caring if he startled the locals. His heart raced in more than just effort and *that* only served to piss him off more. He wasn't scared about fucking up his mission. He was worried. About *her.*

Yeah, he was seriously pissed.

He knew the guys on his team would keep eyes on her location, especially after the chewing out they received yesterday. He had no doubt she would be exactly where they said she was, but Jesus Christ, the moment his gaze found her, she'd be lucky if he didn't wring her damn neck!

"Whoa," Lorenzo said, stepping to the side to avoid getting barreled over by Axle. "What are you—"

The locals she was speaking to shuffled back right as Caitlin looked over her shoulder. She turned around quickly to face him right as he came to a stop inches from her.

"What's going on?" she asked. He could see she was genuinely puzzled by his sudden appearance, but there was also something flashing in her gaze. Irritation.

He glared at her and tried to rein in his emotions. He was losing his shit. Fuck, he hated being anything but methodical. Never in his life had he ever been rash. Not in his personal dealings and sure as hell not in his career.

His comm was firing off as his men were checking in. He needed them to stay in position, so he answered, "False alarm. Do not un-ass."

Caitlin's shoulders relaxed before turning toward the men she'd been speaking to, but most had scattered.

"Hashem," she said, and waved at him. She took a step in the man's direction, but Axle grabbed her arm.

She whirled. "What?" she said, barking the word at him.

He blinked at her, still trying to collect his thoughts. He didn't know what was coming over him, but the thought of her being out of arm's reach was unacceptable.

"You and I," she said, slowly, "are having a talk later about you *letting* me do my job."

"Talk all you want, but from now on, I'm standing right beside you."

She gaped at him. "You're kidding."

"Nope."

"How am I supposed to get anyone to talk about the military strike if I have a military man strapped to my hip?"

"Not my problem."

She dropped the hand that held the mic and stepped closer to him. "This right here is why we're gonna have a conversation later. For now, I need to speak to these people before you up and decide it's time to leave." She turned, and he followed when she started toward Hashem. She glanced over her should once, and he was skilled enough in detecting soft sounds that he didn't miss the quiet, "Asshole."

He'd have to agree, but he was through letting her have her way. She probably didn't think he'd been very forthcoming so far. He had a feeling that would be the gist of their conversation later, but it was high time she figured out just who was in charge here.

———

CAITLIN DIDN'T LEARN anything new on today's excursion, so instead of mentally going over information on their trip back like she'd hoped to be doing, she'd gone over just what she wanted to say to Axle. Her thoughts had been all over the place, though. From cussing him out to pleading with him, she hadn't figured out the best course to take with him once they talked.

And they were going to do just that as soon as they landed. This conversation was long overdue. Hunter had been right. Plus, she couldn't afford another wasted day on this story. She and Axle were both adults. They both had jobs to do.

Once they were back on base and she was far enough away from the noise of the helicopter, she turned to Lorenzo.

"Send me the raw footage you have when you get back to your room. I need to see what I have to work with." She hadn't gotten much from the people, but there was always a chance he'd captured something.

He smiled. "You could always come with me and watch

it. I think you could use a break away from all this to focus on work." His pointed glance at Axle was not missed.

"No more field trips today, kiddos," Axle said, stepping up to them. "We can set you up in a meeting room here if you need to keep working. One big enough for *all* of us."

True to his word, he hadn't left her side since announcing she'd have a new shadow. She almost found it sweet he was so concerned.

Almost.

It just showed her when he got something stuck in his head, he was determined to see it through.

"There's something else I need to take care of," she told Lorenzo. She'd love to go over the material with him, but now wasn't the time. "Go ahead and send me the video from today, and I'll message you with any questions I have."

If they set up in the meeting room right now, Lorenzo would have to wait for her to finish her little chitchat with the stern sailor. That'd be rude of her to ask, but no way did she want a room full of witnesses for her conversation with Axle either. He was too much of a stickler for rank and order when he was around other people, and she needed him to be somewhat understanding to her plight. They needed to be alone if she was going to have any chance at getting through to him.

"How about a drink then?" Lorenzo asked. "I mean, if we're taking a break from work, might as well enjoy it. And you've been working really hard. You deserve some downtime."

She blinked, not sure how to respond. "That's sweet, but the only way I'm getting a break is if I'm in my room." From the moment she left the barracks until she returned, she had to focus on work. Not that she took a break when she was alone in her room either, but if there was a time, it'd be then. She glanced at Axle, sweat beading on his temple. Her gaze traveled down slowly, and she quickly jerked her attention back to Lorenzo before her eyes ate up more. Okay, so she didn't *only* focus on work during the waking hours.

"Well, now, that's a little more like it," Lorenzo said, taking a step toward her.

"Oh for fuck's sake," Axle growled, and raised an arm between them, stopping Lorenzo's advancement. "I gotta watch her twenty-four-seven, and I sure as shit don't wanna suffer through thirty seconds of you humping her leg like a horny stray dog."

Lorenzo turned red. Caitlin gaped at him.

"Er, Commander, the pilot wants to know what time to meet in the morning," one of his guys asked.

"Oh-eight-hundred. Give the locals more time to rise and shine before we show." Then he took Caitlin's arm, pulling her along, but looked over his should as they walked. "Make sure Lorenzo gets safely to his hotel."

"Yes, Sir."

She heard Lorenzo cussing behind her, but she was too stunned to form words. Axle practically dragged her all the way to the barracks. When they neared, he veered to the side of the building, and she yanked her arm loose as soon as they were clear of other people.

"You wanted to talk," he said, and crossed his arms. She knew a fight stance when she saw it.

"What the hell's wrong with you?" she asked. Of all the ways she'd envisioned this conversation starting, that wasn't one of them.

He huffed and ran a hand through his hair. His frustration was palpable, but so was her determination.

"You." He leaned against the wall, bending a knee and propping that foot against it. "You don't listen."

"Ha! My *job* is to listen," she said, pointing at her chest. "I'm very good at it, actually."

"Really? Then why do you have such a hard time doing what I say?"

She took a deep breath, wanting this conversation to be productive and not a battle. "Look. I get you're trying to protect me, and I appreciate it—"

"Sweetheart, I'm not doing this for your benefit. I have orders. Orders," he said again, pushing himself off the wall. He took a step toward her, and her heart raced. There was a fire in his gaze that sparked an echoing answer deep in her core. It excited her. It worried her. All the reasons were the same, but logic didn't have a place. Just when she started to open her mouth, he shook his head, breaking the electric connection and walking a couple feet away from her.

Caitlin shut her eyes briefly and made her way to the wall he'd just vacated. It was either use it to keep herself upright or crumble to the ground. She felt weak in the knees and needed the support that surface would give. Part of her hated this attraction she felt toward him, but she was smart enough to keep it at bay. At least she tried to.

With a fortifying breath, she turned and leaned into the building's façade.

Axle paced.

"I have to be able to do my job," she said slowly in an effort to bring down the combative tone she'd had earlier, and it was the truth. She was here for work.

"Me, too," he said without looking at her. Crap. He wasn't making this easy at all, not that she expected him to.

"I'm a big girl," she said, trying to be funny.

He laughed, but it didn't hold the humor she'd been

shooting for. The husky sound was fuel to that spark she'd felt earlier in the base of her spine.

"Axle," she said, with more authority, trying to both pull his attention back to her and command her own errant thoughts to focus on the task at hand.

He stopped and looked at her finally.

"I understand the danger. Believe me, I've heard all the warnings about working in a war zone. My boss, my dad, my friends. Hell, even the guy I had the hots for gave me a list of do's and don't's."

That look.

If she wasn't already up against the wall, she'd take a step back. The urge to retreat was almost overwhelming because that look told her she was in serious trouble.

Why?

He moved toward her slowly. "The guy you had the hots for?"

Another step.

Uh-oh.

"Umm..."

"He must be pretty important to you if you'll listen to him, but not me. The guy who's actually trying to keep your ass safe."

Holy crap. *Is he jealous?*

There was no doubt she was attracted to him. He was tall, handsome, and protective. Any woman with estrogen would find him sexy. Hell, she wouldn't be surprised if those without did too. She figured the interest wasn't one-sided. There'd been a few times when he looked at her, touched her, that seemed he struggled too. Even if there hadn't been those moments, she was funny and not awful to look at. She'd had her share of advances from the opposite sex. Lorenzo had just asked her for drinks, and she was filthy from working in the dust all day. But this? The possession radiating off Axle screamed more than a passing fancy.

"I've known him since I was a kid," she tried to explain.

"So you two have a history."

It wasn't a question, but she felt the need to answer anyway. "No, I mean, yes. I trust him, but no, we don't have *history* history." He continued taking slow steps toward her as a predator stalking its prey would, so she spoke faster. "I grew up in a really small town, and he's my best friend's brother. She freaked out when she found out I got an assignment outside the wire, and he just so happened to be there when I told her. He's the one who got you assigned to protect me."

That stopped him.

It stopped everything.

No more advancement. No more jealousy.

No more heat.

"What's his name?" She opened her mouth to answer, but something told her Hunter needed to stay out of this. *Should've thought of that two seconds ago, dummy.* "Caitlin," he said, dragging out her name.

"It's not important."

"The hell it isn't. I want a name."

"That's not what I needed to talk to you about." Jesus, she had to get this conversation back on track immediately. "I wanted to talk to you about you letting me do my job. We need to work together, find some kinda compromise that lets me work on my story without unnecessary setbacks."

He stopped right in front of her. "You don't get to call the shots."

"And I don't report to you."

His smile was slow and full of self-confidence. "You'll do whatever I say."

"This is what I'm talking about. You're not the boss of me." Gah, she sounded like a twelve-year-old. "But I think we can find some common ground here. Something that'll let me get good material for my piece while you still do your thing."

"And how do you propose we do that?"

Her eyes popped, but she quickly masked her surprise at him willing to compromise. "Um, for starters, you can talk to me about the agenda before it's set in stone. That'd help me better plan the segments and schedule time to work when we're back."

"Anything else?"

"Yeah, you can stand several feet away when I'm interviewing witnesses. It weirds out the locals when you're right there, and it freezes up other military personnel too. You're intimidating."

"Good."

She sighed. "But it's counterproductive."

"I'll work with you on the agenda. No promises, though. It's not like scheduling an appointment with a doctor. I don't have a lot of leeway to begin with."

"I understand that."

"I won't compromise on your safety."

"Axle—"

"But," he stressed, "I'll try another formation technique tomorrow, and we'll see how that goes. That's the best I can offer."

If she was honest with herself, she knew it was probably the best she was going get out of him. "Thank you."

His face suddenly hardened, and his hand quickly landed on each side of her, caging her against the wall, trapping her where she stood. "Give. Me. His. Name."

Crap. She'd hoped he was going to drop that. She

couldn't tell him who Hunter was. What if he'd over-stepped in getting Axle assigned to her protection? She didn't want him to get in trouble. She figured Axle would find out eventually, but hopefully not until this assignment was over.

She shook her head, trying to think of what to say, of how to stall.

"Caitlin, I'm not letting you go until I get his name."

"I don't see how that's—"

"Do you know how many years I've studied interrogation techniques? Do you have any idea how skilled I am at torture? How long I can go without food or sleep?"

This wall of muscle meant to scare her. She knew that, but she was not going to take the bait. "No, why would I? I don't know if you're a dog or a cat person. I don't know if you're married." Then she quickly added, "Hell, I don't even know how old you are." She shrugged, trying to make light of her questions.

He smiled again, and it was sexy as sin.

"I love dogs." His head lowered, and his heat bathed the side of her neck. "I'm single." Her air became very shallow and goosebumps exploded on her skin. "And I'm old enough to know how to get exactly what I want, darlin'."

The world spun, and she squeezed her eyes shut to help get her bearings. She could feel him all over, and he wasn't even touching her. How was that even possible?

His nose nuzzled her hair and his hot breath tickled her ear, "Tell me." His lips very lightly brushed her lobe, and a shiver rocked through her. "Give it to me."

Jesus, at this moment, she'd give him the shirt of her back. *Hell yeah I would.* And her bra...and her pants...

She swayed into him. "Ishmael," she whispered. It

wasn't a complete lie. Hunter had called himself that on his profile, and technically, *Hunter* wasn't his name either.

Axle pressed into her then and buried his head in her hair. God, she didn't know what was going on with him, but she didn't want to be reasonable anymore. She reached for him, needing more contact, but in that moment, he pulled back slightly. She gripped the sides of the wall instead and immediately missed his warmth. When she opened her eyes, he was staring back, watching her. His gaze was almost soft, but his jaw twitched as if he was gritting his teeth, the two responses at war with each other.

He was battling himself.

After what seemed like an eternity, he took a step back, then another, putting more distance between them, severing the connection that hadn't just been physical. "I'll have Acker bring you some chow, so you can work."

Was he going to ignore what happened just now? It wasn't the first intense moment they'd had since meeting, but there was no denying something was going on between them. She couldn't explain it herself, but she was done trying to. "You're just gonna walk away?" she asked, mainly out of shock, but with a little bit of anger thrown in. "Got nothing to say about what just happened?"

"Nothing happened," he said flatly. "Get some sleep. Don't work all night. We've got another long day tomorrow."

She laughed, a quick mirthless sound. "Right. You're absolutely right." She moved then, needing to get away. "But I can't work right now. Think I'm gonna take Lorenzo up on his drink offer." Drowning her sorrows sounded like a perfect idea right now.

He grabbed her arm, stopping her. "I did you a favor earlier. Don't be stupid."

Whether or not he saved her from Lorenzo was irrelevant. "I don't need anything from you." She yanked her arm free with unnecessary force and stomped away. She fought the urge to look over her shoulder to see if he followed, but once she reached the ATV and climbed in, she saw he'd stayed rooted in place, watching her.

Only now he was on the phone. Probably calling in reinforcements since he was too chickenshit to face her himself.

She reached the chow hall, doubtful there'd be a nice wine selection, but willing to take whatever they had. Some men were already there eating, and they glanced up at her when she walked in. She gave a few of them a flat smile before looking around.

"I hear you can use this," someone said from behind her.

She turned around. "He calls and you come running," she said to Brooks.

"That *is* how it works." He raised an eyebrow and then lifted a bottle of whisky.

"Wow, I'm surprised he approved this," she said, grabbing it.

Brooks chuckled. "Believe it or not, he likes to pick his battles."

She rolled her eyes and walked to the drink station for a cup. She grabbed one and a soft drink, and took a seat nearby. Brooks sat across from her right when Acker materialized with a tray of food. He put it on the table in front of her and stepped back.

"Right on cue," she said to him, and then added, "I'm not hungry." She got to work mixing her beverage.

"If you don't eat, I have to tell the boss," Acker said, almost jokingly, but she knew he was giving her fair warning.

"Fine," she breathed. She took two bites, gulped her drink, and winced at how strong it was. "Happy?"

"Damn skippy."

She poured a little more soda into her glass. "Food's not bad, but the wine selection is lacking. Three and a half stars," she said to the man in front of her, joking a *Yelp* review.

Brooks laughed. "It's definitely not Salsa Night at Kandahar Airfield."

She smiled. "Right? I got to experience that when working on a story last year. Totally different vibe."

"This area isn't known for its nightlife."

"I've noticed." She took a few more bites of her food. She hadn't been hungry, but once she started eating, her stomach cheered her on. She glanced at Acker to make sure he saw she was being a good little girl and eating her dinner, but he'd left. Or he was standing somewhere incognito, watching her from a distance. Probably the second one.

She focused on her dinner companion. He was cute, but there was no attraction. There was only one man she wanted, and that was a problem. She took another sip. "What's your name?" she asked. "Because it feels weird calling you by your last name."

"Brooks is my first name, ma'am."

"Oh. I just figured it was your last since everyone around here tends to favor those."

"My commanding officer does."

"I've only heard him call you Brooks," she said, taking another bite.

"Landry isn't my normal CO. This is a special operation."

Right. "Well, it's nice to meet you." She reached across

the table, and he shook her hand. "Caitlin Cooper. At least you're not a dick too."

"It's a pleasure," he said before releasing her. "And I have my moments."

"Don't we all, Brooks. Don't we all."

She continued eating her meal and sipping her soda... the one in the can, not the one mixed in the glass. The few sips of alcohol had given her a slight buzz, and that was more than enough to take the edge off. She didn't want to get shit-faced, or rather, she didn't want a doozy of a hang-over tomorrow. There was no telling if Axle would keep his word and be more accommodating or if he'd continue being completely and totally unreasonable. She couldn't take the risk of not being able to focus with whatever time he allowed her to interview the townspeople.

Brooks ask her a couple of questions about her job and growing up while she ate. By the time she was finished eating, she knew more about him than any other person there. When she rose to leave, he stood. "Thank you for the company."

"My pleasure."

"No, it was mine," she said. "I think you're the first person who hasn't been irritated at my presence. It's nice to make a friend."

"Well, you're welcome," he said, and it looked like he might be blushing.

"Do you know if Lorenzo is still on base?" She checked her watch. If he was, she could meet up with him and get in a couple of hours of viewing footage before she turned in for the night.

"No, ma'am. He was escorted back to his hotel."

"Crap. Okay. Guess I'll head back to my room then."

"Yes, ma'am."

"None of that *ma'am* business. We look like we're the same age." She laughed.

Brooks drove her to the barracks, and she waved him off before entering. She glanced at Axle's closed door, but didn't veer off course to her own room. They were probably alone in this building and that possibility stirred her anger toward him. It was irrational, she knew. Not the anger part —she had every right to be irritated with him—but the thought they could be alone here, and he'd still avoid her.

Just as well. She needed to work, but she felt too keyed up to concentrate on her story. A shower. That'd help. The hot water would relax her and get her mind where it needed to be.

On work.

Not Axle.

She kicked off her shoes and shed some of her clothes. When she walked toward the dresser to get clean pajamas, something sharp suddenly dug into her foot. She gasped and hopped on one foot the last couple of steps. She leaned into the dresser to support herself, and grabbing her injured foot, she looked down to see what had been the culprit.

She saw red.

Not blood, oh no. That was not the red clouding her gaze.

It was anger.

Pure and hot.

CHAPTER TEN

Axle sat at the edge of his bed with his laptop open, waiting for his sister's call. His elbows rested on his knees, head in his hands, as he tried to shake off the enigma that was Caitlin Cooper.

"You're fucking losing it," he muttered to himself.

He wasn't one to mess up. Years of training and missions had honed his skills and perfected his senses, but inside of a week with this woman, he was making rookie mistakes.

He'd torn out of the village the other day when she'd just been trying to do her job. They hadn't been scheduled to leave for another hour, but the second he realized Caitlin wasn't where she was supposed to be, he'd gone ape-shit. On the surface, he'd come across as a stern asshole because years in special ops honed him to function in the worst of situations. But on the inside? He'd freaked out. He knew she wouldn't have had time to go far. He knew his guys had eyes on her, too. He also knew it didn't take long to make a clean, undetected kill.

If that wasn't bad enough, he'd lost sight of her again today.

A litany of cuss words ghosted out of his mouth. He'd lost her. It had been short, and she'd been okay, but he'd still lost her. Again. Axle knew it happened all the time with other people, but he'd never lost sight of anyone before Caitlin. He was a sniper, for crying out loud. Keeping his eyes peeled was his goddamn job.

But oh, that wasn't the end of his stupidity. When Lorenzo made yet another pass at her, Axle couldn't sit there and listen. She'd turned him down already, but the dude wouldn't take no for an answer. The man lacked any skills when it came to reading women, and Axle had been about two seconds away from giving Lightweight a personal lesson.

Yeah, rookie mistakes...both professional and personal.

His laptop sounded an incoming call, pulling him out of his downward spiral, and he clicked to accept it.

"Hey, Sis."

"Bubby," she said excitedly. "I miss your face!" She wrinkled her nose. "You could've at least put a shirt on."

He chuckled. "I miss you, too, and it's hot as balls here." His sister had seen him running around in boxers, but he grabbed the thin sheet and tucked it under his arms to cover himself a little. "There." He leaned closer and tried assessing her through the screen. "How're you feeling?"

She rolled her eyes. "Are you going to ask me that every time we talk?"

"You were shot. That's not something people tend to get over right away ...especially how it all went down."

She sighed. "I'm fine. Taking an extended leave of absence while I think about my future."

"So you're not *feeling* fine at all."

"Physically, I'm golden. But mentally I'm..."

When she trailed off and didn't say anything else for several seconds, Axle said, "Fucked?"

She laughed. "Yeah, that. I'm not sure I want to be an agent anymore."

He let out a breath. It wasn't a shock, but he'd hoped this wasn't a path she was considering. "Don't let that asshole steal your career. You've worked damned hard to get it."

"I know, and I miss the challenge sometimes, but I've been enjoying working at the garage."

"I thought Dad closed it," he said, frowning at her. Last he'd heard, their dad had retired.

"Yeah, he *sold* it," she said, smiling. "I didn't think he'd agree, but he did."

"What?" He reared back. "Someone bought that shithole?"

Shelby giggled. "Yep. Already leveled it. Going to put in one of those outside shopping centers."

"Well, hell. There goes Plan B." Working at the car shop had been an option for him if he decided not to reup his military contract. So much for that.

"What do you mean?"

"It means, I need this mission to go a lot fucking better than it has if I want to advance my career because retiring from service and living out my years as a mechanic is no longer an option."

"You're thinking about quitting?" she asked with a raised voice. "Why didn't you say anything?"

"I think about it whenever it's time to reup. *Every*body does."

"Yeah, but if I'd have known you were even thinking of working at the shop, I wouldn't have okayed the purchase."

"Dad talked to *you* about it?" Why hadn't he talked to Axle? He knew it was misogynistic to think their father should've talk to him first, but Axle was not only his son, but he was the oldest. It was a male dominated industry. The only female to ever work at the garage was Shelby, and it wasn't as if she'd chosen to work in that field once she was old enough to make her own decisions about her life.

"Don't get all righteous with me. I've been back home way more times than you have. When's the last time you even stepped foot in the garage, much less rotated a tire in it?"

She was right, and he damn well knew it. "Sorry," he said sheepishly. "Just hadn't considered it was sold when he said he retired."

She huffed, obviously still irritated, not that he blamed her. "Anyway," she said slowly. "I thought you'd be happy Dad gets to live his golden years on a fishing boat and not underneath a greasy car."

"Yeah, of course. It's just a lot, you know?" He hoped like hell their dad didn't get screwed on the deal, but the land wasn't worth much anyway. Axle should be happy he was able to get something out of it. The few times he'd visited recently, he'd noticed the area had started to look shabby. His father didn't get customers because of location, that was for sure. "The poor sap who bought it will probably regret it."

"I hope not because he can be grouchy when business doesn't go as planned." Her smile was tender, and his neck prickled.

"What the hell does that mean?" But he knew. Oh, yeah, he fucking knew. "Your boyfriend bought it."

"Boyfriend," she said with a smirk. "That still sounds weird."

"Goddamnit, Shelby. You let some man you're fucking buy our family business."

"He's not just some guy I'm screwing."

"No, he was a man you were paid to investigate and then started banging."

She went quiet, but the look she gave him was anything but meek. "Watch it. Just because you're my brother and can get away with talking shit others can't does *not* mean I'm going to sit here and listen to you act like I'm some whore."

"I didn't call you that," he said, lifting his hands in a placating gesture.

"It was implied. The feds paid me to sleep with him and now that I'm not on their payroll, Mason is shelling out the bucks. Yeah, it's exactly what you meant."

He sighed. "I'm sorry. Really. I know you're not a whore. Even if you were hooking up with everyone south of the Mason-Dixon-Line, I still wouldn't think that."

She tilted her head to the side and gave him a crooked smile. "Did you say *Mason* on purpose?"

He shook his head, avoiding a chuckle. "I should probably get used to hearing that name."

"Yeah, you should." She smiled fully then.

"Does he treat you right?" he asked.

"Depends on your definition of that." She wagged her eyebrows.

He lifted his hand, blocking her. "Ahh, I don't wanna know that."

She laughed, clearly enjoying his discomfort. Axle didn't say anything, wanting her to get all the showmanship out of her system. When she got her humor under control, she said, "So, as I was saying earlier, I've been working at the garage...the one in *Arkansas*. I like it, and Mason has been very supportive while I take this time to think about my options."

"Oh." He wasn't sure how he felt about that. "I knew you got attached to those guys when you were put on assignment there, but I didn't think you'd gotten this close to them."

"There's a lot you don't know about them."

His radio crackled, drawing his attention. "Charlie heading into the barracks," Acker said.

Axle picked it up, replied his acknowledgment of the message, and put it back on its charging base. He heard the door to the main entry and then the one across the hall.

"What was that?" Shelby asked.

"Caitlin's back." He looked at his closed door.

"Caitlin?" she asked slowly. "Why did you say it like that?" She cocked a brow.

"Like what?"

"Like you *love* her," she said in a taunting tone she perfected around kindergarten. Ever the bratty little sister.

"Jesus Christ, you can be such a nuisance."

"More than you know." She grimaced. "Which is why I asked you not to hate me."

Oh yeah, the message she'd sent him shortly after he'd arrived here. "What did you do?" he asked, but the answer was everywhere.

"Caitlin is friends with one of the guys at the shop. He wanted her protected, and I might have reminded him you were a SEAL."

He shut his eyes and gritted his teeth to keep from yelling at her.

"I said I was sorry. It seemed really important to him, and you're the only man who's recently been to a warzone that I know. I wanted to be helpful."

"C'mon, Shel. First you ask me to look into Mason's brother—"

"*Oooh*, did you find something out about Caleb?"

"And now you're pulling strings, messing with my structure," he said over her question. "No, I haven't found anything out about Caleb Showalter. How the hell am I going to have time to do that when you get me yanked out of downtime to work another operation?"

"Look, I wasn't sure if there was anything you could do to help with Caitlin, but once I mentioned it, the other guys agreed you could be useful. Heck, when I said we should probably find someone already stationed there instead of relocating you, Gauge said you'd be perfect and immediately started making calls."

"And Ishmael? I bet he just fucking loved knowing Caitlin was going to be protected by a SEAL."

"Who's Ishmael?" She frowned at him.

Axle blinked and, in that moment, reality clicked. Instead of answering her, he asked, "What's the name of the man who instigated this?"

"Um." She hesitated, and Axle had no patience for any stalling tactics. He told himself it was because he wanted a name for the person who started this, but he knew the real reason. Whoever the man was had meant something to Caitlin, and he cared enough about her to uproot lives to make sure she was protected.

That rankled, but what pissed him off was that Caitlin had lied to his face about the other man.

"Give me his name, Shelby. You ask me to help with your lover's brother. You didn't give me a choice to help you now. I can keep naming shit I've done for you over the years without so much as a question. The least you can do is give me a name."

She nodded slowly. "Hunter Anderson."

A door slammed, jerking his attention. What was Caitlin doing? Was she trying to sneak away? They were on a base, for Christ's sake, and if she was attempting to leave without him knowing, she sure was hell wasn't being quiet about it.

"I gotta go." He didn't let Shelby respond before shutting the laptop. He grabbed the shirt he'd discarded and took a step toward the door, but it flew open before he reached it.

He almost winced at the anger rolling off Caitlin. Damn, but if she wasn't the most beautiful woman he'd ever laid eyes on. Even angry. There was just something about this woman.

And he hated himself for thinking of her like that. Yes, he was a straight, virile man, but he was also a special operator in the military who knew how to keep his dick in his pants, even if his cock refused his orders too.

"Came to say sorry for lying to me about Ishmael?" he asked.

"I got your apology right here."

She yanked her arm back and swung in his direction. He didn't see what she had in her hand, but he deflected whatever it was she threw at him. She yelled as she charged. Pissed off women weren't part of his combat training, but his skills kicked in anyway. He grabbed her arm and spun her around, holding her by her midsection against his body. She kicked out, her foot connecting with the door, making it slam so hard the walls shook. She gasped out a sound of pain, and only then did he notice she didn't have on any shoes. He didn't have time to think beyond that because the infuriated woman had managed to gain enough force when she connected with the door that he lost his footing. Axle tripped over his boots, and he landed on his back on the bed, still holding her to him. She flailed, but he refused to lessen his grip.

"*Caitlin.*"

"I hate you!"

All right then. He twisted to his side and managed to turn her so that her back was on the mattress, and he rolled on top of her. He grabbed her arms and pinned them above her head.

She growled, and he slapped his halfway free hand over her mouth. It wasn't really the best position to be in, her beneath him, writhing, but damn. What choice did he have? "Would you calm down?" he said through his teeth. Her movements were making him stir until he became excruciatingly hard.

She slowed, but her breath sawed in and out of her body, forcing her breasts to mash against him. Jesus, he did not need to be thinking about her body when she was pinned beneath him.

On a bed.

While he lost yet another battle with his wayward dick.

After several agonizing seconds, she completely relaxed, and he chanced moving his hand. When she didn't scream, he pulled it away to prop himself up a little higher, creating some space between their heaving bodies. Though his hadn't been because of exertion.

At least not yet.

No. He had to focus here. He looked to the side, willing his mind to work, and saw the object she'd hurled at him.

"If you get this pissed when you run out of ink, I'd hate to see how you handle road rage."

She glared wordlessly.

"When I told you it was a weapon, I didn't think you'd try using it on me."

Still nothing. And he was glad her hands were secured far away from his gun.

"Are you always a jerk when you're attracted to someone?"

He sighed, dropping his forehead on top of hers, losing the hardest battle of his life—resisting her. "No," he breathed.

The seconds ticked by, and somehow, he found himself closer to her. He was strong enough to hold himself up, but the strength currently in control wasn't led by his external abilities, overriding the power in his arms. And he'd quickly learned that he had no mental or emotional control when it came to this woman. It was some other force within calling the shots.

"You've been a jerk since I got here," she said, but there wasn't any fire in her words.

He had his eyes closed. A last-ditch effort to put some distance between them. He knew if he opened them now, he would be a goner.

"I'm sorry," he said, and he meant it. Completely. "I can't explain it. Fuck, I wish I could, but you drive me *insane*, baby."

Her breath bathed his face, and his mouth dropped closer to inhale the luscious scent that was her. All her. He shouldn't be doing this. He should not be holding her down on his bed. He knew this. He fucking *knew* this.

He couldn't move away. Every time he shifted, thinking he was creating space, he was drawing nearer to her.

"Axle," she breathed. His name leaving her mouth caused her lips to brush against his. *That* was how close they'd gotten.

And it wasn't close enough.

On a strangled groan, he slammed his mouth over hers, his tongue diving in to the hot cavern of her sweet, sweet mouth.

Her moan vibrated against his chest before it reached his ears, and the sensations of feeling her acquiescence in addition to hearing it? It wasn't dropping a flame onto gasoline. It was a bomb detonating, obliterating his senses and fueling him to take her, claim her, mark her. A feeling unlike any other he'd ever experienced before. And he'd had his fair share of women. But not like this.

Never like this.

Unable to stop his actions, Axle rolled over her fully and thrust his jeans-clad cock between her thighs. Without stopping his assault on her mouth, he released her wrists and grabbed both hands into his, lacing their fingers together, still holding them above her head. Somewhere in the back of his mind, he knew he was dry-humping her like some horny teenager waiting for the green light to go further, and he was far from that. But to move away and remove her clothes meant to stop touching her.

He couldn't. Not yet.

So he kissed her, fucked her mouth with his tongue, as he slammed his aching cock against her over and over. If he kept this up, he'd explode in his pants, but he couldn't find that thing in his brain that made him care. He'd resisted this woman for days, hadn't been able to think clearly when she was around him. And now was no different. Still no reason. There was no finesse, no gentle kissing or caressing, gently encouraging her to give herself to him. He was a power-house that had been pushed beyond all sanity, reduced to carnal instincts. If he shifted, she could move or someone could swoop in and take her from him, and his animalistic need to keep her pinned for his pleasure blocked out all rational thought.

It wasn't until she tugged on her arms that he pushed through the lusty fog and released her hands. Still not waiting to move away, he gripped the sides of her face the moment his palms were available as he continued to plunder her mouth. Her hands were free, so if she pushed him away now, he'd muster all his strength to rear back and away from her. It'd kill him, but he'd do it if she wanted.

He needn't worry about that. Caitlin's legs wrapped around him, and she thrust up as he plowed against her, her hands grasping at his bare back. That skin-on-skin contact, no barrier between, felt so good he had to have more, the desire finally stronger than the need to stay where he'd been the last several minutes.

His lips trailed down her throat as he pulled down the strap of her tank top, his mouth following the path he forged as he wrenched it and her bra low enough to expose a breast. He wasted no time claiming her nipple, laving and sucking it as if couldn't get enough, and when it *wasn't* enough, he shoved his hand under her and pulled her tighter against him as he devoured her.

And still he needed more.

The incoherent sounds coming from her as he feasted on her body drove him mad. Axle grabbed the other strap with his free hand and yanked it down to free her other breast. He heard material rip, and instead of cooling his ardor, the sound threw him into a frenzy of passion. He delved to the newly exposed nipple and ravished it as he shoved his hands between them and unfastened her pants. With only enough patience to unzip until he had enough room, he slipped his hand underneath her partially unzipped pants and into her panties.

The moment his finger slipped between her wet folds, she gasped and breathed out, "Yesss."

He lifted up then, finally able to pull his mouth off her to look down at the beautiful, flushed creature below him. He panted, his finger exploring slowly. When he dipped it inside her, his head bowed, overcome with momentary weakness at how drenched she was for him. He did this to her, the knowledge a heady punch. Then he grazed her clit, and Caitlin's knees slammed against his thighs as if she was trying to close her legs. The action had been involuntary, the confusion of pleasure controlling her limbs, he knew. But he was cocky enough to revel in the knowledge that *his* powerful legs between hers held her open to him no matter how her body instinctively reacted.

She clutched the arm he used to brace himself over her. Her other hand gripped his shoulder, her nails digging into his flesh. He didn't know if she warred with herself to push him away or pull him closer, but the bite of pain she dealt him only fueled him. If she wanted to stop, he would. There was no doubt he'd respect her wishes no matter what, but no way in hell was he going to make it easy for her to deny what was happening. He moved his finger over her clit, light and fast. Her thighs kept flexing as her knees squeezed against his outer legs repeatedly, and still he watched her eyes.

Until they rolled back in her head.

He slowed his caress of her most sensitive spot, determined to drag out her orgasm. Because she was about to; he could see it in the way her skin darkened, her breaths growing shallow, her hips flexing toward him, and there was nothing he wanted in life more than to watch this woman come apart.

"Don't stop," she breathed, and grabbed his chest with both hands, her nails digging into his pecs.

"Never." But he didn't increase his tempo, his movements almost languid as he watched her.

"Faster," she begged. Not only had he considered not giving her what she asked, he almost ventured away and into her pussy to prolong it even more, but then she said, "Please, Axle. *Please.*" Power surged in him at how desperate she was for him, and he knew then no matter what he wanted, he couldn't deny her anything. His finger sped, moving faster over her clit as he bent closer to her, ignoring the pain of her fingernails. He wanted to be as close to her body as he could when she flew.

"Oh, God."

"Give it to me, Caitlin. C'mon, baby." His forehead dropped to hers, sweat slipping from his temple onto her. His whole hand vibrated inside her panties as his middle finger ghosted over her clit with lightning speed.

She convulsed and sucked in all the air around them. Axle's mouth slammed down on top of hers, capturing her scream. Her hands fisted in his hair, her hips pumping as she rode the high, and he was so close to coming just by feeling and watching that he almost didn't care if he got inside of her first.

Almost.

When she relaxed below him, Axle surged up and yanked her pants down. Before taking his off, he reached into the small nightstand for a condom, because the moment his dick was free, he wouldn't stop to secure protection. He unbuttoned his pants, but the sight of Caitlin whipping her shirt and bra off momentarily stunned him.

"You're so fucking beautiful." The naked woman on his bed blushed at his words, and he enjoyed seeing the color bloom on parts of her body he hadn't gotten to gaze upon when she'd been embarrassed by something these last few days. Then she licked her lips, and his temporary paralysis disappeared, followed by the rest of his clothes.

He climbed on the bed one-handed as he held the condom with the other and ripped it open with his teeth. He rolled it on and grabbed her thigh instead as he nestled himself between her legs. He came over her, and she reached between them to grab his cock.

"Fuuuck." He wasn't going to last long. No matter how sweet it was feeling her hand engulf him, he had to knock it away and take control. He was too close to heaven to risk losing the chance to feel it. He grabbed his dick and pushed into her. The moment he was inside enough to let go, he shoved his hands under her back, grabbed her shoulders to anchor her, and pushed into her sweet body. He wasn't fast, but he was unrelenting, not stopping until fully seated.

"So good," she breathed.

He groaned as he pulled back and plunged into her, this time faster, harder. "Can't go slow." Part of him wanted to. Wanted to drag this out and make it last all night, but there was no way on this planet he'd be able to find the willpower to do that. Not this time.

"Don't."

He withdrew until almost completely out and plowed into her again as he took possession of her mouth. Caitlin's legs wound around his back as he thrust into her faster, harder. Her hands clutched his face, his shoulders, scratching his back. They were everywhere she could reach, spurring him with each new touch.

Axle wasn't sure when he passed the point of no return. *You passed that the moment you laid eyes on her.* That thought sent a little shock through him, but he pushed it away to focus on the now.

He ripped his mouth away and buried his face in the crook of her neck. "Jesus, you're so fucking tight." And he wasn't just saying that. She was squeezing the life out of him as she rocked against him, giving back as good as she got.

His name left her lips in a chant, a benediction on a sensual loop. He felt her walls clench around him, and he wanted to shout his victory at getting to feel her come around him this time.

Her pussy seized and then spasmed as she screamed, but unlike earlier, he didn't silence her. Instead, he reared back, and fucked her with short jabs, making her breasts bounce with effort, and slipped his hand between them to play with her clit to force her ecstasy to last as long as he could.

But when she opened her eyes to look at him, he was gone. Totally done for. He grabbed her hips and held her so tightly he knew he'd leave marks on her otherwise flawless skin, but he couldn't control his strength right now. He pushed into her with so much power, and fucked her so savagely, feeling too exposed, so fucking *raw* in this moment. He drilled her into the goddamn mattress and still he couldn't get deep enough.

She clutched at him, coming again or coming still; he didn't know and was too far gone to give a damn at this point because his cock had taken over and was on a mission to find the best release of his existence. Finally—*finally*—his climax slammed into him with the full force of his ministrations and he roared, spilling himself into the condom. Giving all he had to her.

And losing himself completely in the process.

CHAPTER ELEVEN

Sunlight shone through the barrack's window, waking Caitlin. She smiled at how boneless she felt, until reality crashed around her, reminding her why she felt so deliciously sore.

I slept with Axle last night.

Okay, so there hadn't been any sleeping going on. He'd rocked her world well past dinner time and into the early morning hours. After the first time, they'd lain there and talked until she'd rubbed her hand across his belly, causing him to stir. Without any preamble, she'd grabbed a condom, put it on him, and rode him until they both came. Later, she'd been looking at map of the country on his wall, talking about his time in the military and how many tours he'd served in Afghanistan. They'd both talked about living in Georgia, and he'd said he wanted to return when he got out, but his dad's shop had been sold. She'd mentioned how short her time was on this trip, but she hadn't gotten to elaborate on her plans because when those words left her lips, she'd suddenly found herself pinned against that very poster with Axle taking her from behind. She hadn't even had time to spread her legs for better access. He just put his on the outside of hers, fisted her hair with one hand, and clawed at her hip with the other as he fucked her. There hadn't even been enough room between the wall and herself for him to reach around and touch her, so when she'd come from penetration alone, it had shocked her. Sure, it had happened to her before, but it wasn't common, and she'd already come with him each time without him touching her. She didn't know if it was because she wanted him just that badly or if it was because it was the thrill of the forbidden.

Probably both. Fraternizing *was* against the rules, but technically, she wasn't in the military. Besides, just because it was against the rules didn't mean it didn't happen.

Boy, did it ever happen.

They hadn't stopped their sexual escapade even when they both had been too wrung out to hardly move, though they'd tried. He'd even taken her to the shower and washed her body for her so they could get some rest. But the sight of Axle naked and wet from the water sluicing off his chiseled frame had her dropping to her knees and taking him into her mouth. She'd been determined to make him come that way, but he'd hooked his hands under her arms and hoisted her up his body. He fucked her against the shower stall as spray from the faucet pelted them. Right after she came, he pulled out and came on her belly. It had been the only time they'd done it without a condom, although they'd discussed their health and history and the fact she was on birth control after he mauled her against the map. She smiled as the memory played in her head again. He'd told her he almost took her bare then. She'd been surprised he'd still had his wits about him to think of protection and having the responsible talk.

After he'd taken her in the shower and washed her a

second time, Axle carried her to her room where he'd tucked her in. She had felt a little pang of sadness that he hadn't taken her back to *his* room, but she'd hadn't had time to dwell on it. Unable to fight exhaustion, she'd fallen right to sleep. Maybe that had been the reason why he hadn't wanted to sleep with her in his arms. He probably knew they wouldn't get any sleep at all if they tempted fate. As it was, they'd missed dinner.

Caitlin rolled to the side, the sunlight blinding her.

"Oh, shit." She tossed the covers off and sat up. They were scheduled to leave later this morning than when they usually did, but the light coming in told her it was obviously much later than eight o'clock. She reached for her phone to check the time and hesitated with a smile when she saw Axle's tactical pen resting on top of a note on her night-stand. There was also a breakfast sandwich wrapped in plastic and a bottle of water. Her phone forgotten, she retrieved his message and read it.

Our flight has been grounded. I got to meet with my superior this morning. I scheduled a conference room for you to work in with your cameraman. Acker and Haverty are positioned outside your room and will be with you until I'm finished. Follow their orders, Caitlin. I mean it. P.S. Now you know the full hidden power of this pen. For the love of God, don't throw it at another man.

She giggled. It wasn't as if it was cupid's arrow. It was a pen—a scary-looking pen, but still a pen. Then again, she had been totally pissed at him last night when she'd stormed into his room, and the moment she'd thrown it at him, their gloves...and shortly thereafter, their clothes...had come off. Maybe there was a little power behind it. She smiled as she looked at it, lost in thought over each time she'd been near Axle since landing.

She stayed in her blissful bubble as she twirled it around in her fingers until her bladder demanded attention, so she put it down to take care of her morning business. After she washed up, and donned some loungewear, she grabbed the breakfast sandwich and ate while pulling out and booting up her laptop. Yesterday hadn't been as productive as she'd hoped—well, not with work—and she needed to play catch-up this morning. When Axle found her later today, she doubted she'd be able to think clearly with him in the same room.

A soft knock sounded, and her heart took off. She leaped from the bed and yanked the door open. Her wide smile faltered when the military man on the other side wasn't the tall, dark, and sexy one she'd been eager to see.

"Well, good morning," Acker said with a smile. She wanted to glare at him, but she couldn't make her lips turn down. "Mr. Ricci is in the Eastside meeting room. When you're ready, I'll escort you."

"Okay, thanks." She should have guessed when Axle noted he'd secured a room for her to work in that he'd have the same message relayed to Lorenzo. "Give me five minutes."

"Yes, ma'am." He backed away, and she shut the door. She changed into more appropriate clothes, shoved her feet into her boots, stowed her laptop, and grabbed the case. She'd also grabbed Axle's tactical pen and stuffed it in the side pocket. He'd left it, so it wasn't as if he *needed* it.

"So is Acker your last name?" she asked as they made their way outside. She didn't want to assume like she had with Brooks.

"Yes, ma'am. Alec Acker. My CO calls me AA. I didn't like it at first because my Pop was an alcoholic, but I gotta say, it sure does irritate the other men in my unit something awful when I'm addressed as *Alpha Alpha* over the radio." He winked at her. "Like I'm so alpha they gotta say it twice."

She giggled. Again with the giggling, but her mood was so light this morning, she was embracing her inner schoolgirl.

"You sure do have a pretty laugh there."

She looked up at him. He was adorable. Tall, green eyes, deep dimples. He was just the type of man she'd go gaga over back home. But when she looked up at him, she felt nothing but general female appreciation for his male beauty.

"I bet the girls just eat you up," she said with a smile.

The light in his eyes dimmed a little, and she wondered what caused that. "No, ma'am."

She nudged his shoulder as they walked toward the ATV parked out front. "Sounds like you haven't met the right kind of women."

He didn't say anything, and she dropped it, not wanting to pry. "You seem to be doing better this morning. Guess you needed some last night." He started the vehicle and headed down the road.

She gaped at him. "What?"

"The whisky," he said, a little puzzled. "You were mad at the world last night and then you drank a little." He briefly looked at her. "Unless you drank more than Brooks reported."

"Oh," she said, fighting a grin. "No. Just a little. But what I got definitely helped." She lost the battle with her lips then. They were pointing to the sky.

He looked at her like she was crazy, and well, she probably was. She didn't care. They spent the rest of the quick ride to the building in silence.

When she walked into the meeting room, Lorenzo jumped up, startling her.

"Where have you been?"

"Umm..." That was a loaded question. She wasn't sure if he was asking where she'd been since yesterday or just today. He probably meant since this morning. She needed to quit thinking everybody who looked at her could tell she'd had sex with Axle. "I overslept. Sorry."

"I emailed you the footage *yesterday*. I haven't heard back," he said with a little edge to his voice.

"I was pretty tired last night," she partially lied. Tiredness hadn't come until much, much later.

"You haven't watched it?" he asked, his eyes popping. The worried sound in his voice had the hair on the back of her neck standing.

"No."

"Come here." He waved her over as he walked to his laptop. "You're not going to believe this."

"What?" she asked, dropping her bag on the table and walking around.

"We've got something. And it's big."

———

AXLE STOOD at ease in front of Burge's desk. The Major Lieutenant had summoned him early this morning, seeking an update on Axle's assignment. There had been an attack in the village where they'd visited yesterday, and they'd been prohibited from traveling to the region today until a team sent to survey the area returned with their report.

Standing in his temporary CO's office, he'd given a rundown of the events that occurred since Caitlin arrived, leaving out one damaging piece of intel—the fact that he'd made love to the woman in question repeatedly over the course of several hours last night.

He wanted nothing more than to find her right now, haul her back to bed, and have his wicked way with her until she couldn't walk. It was Neanderthal of him to feel so possessive of the woman who turned him inside out.

And she did. Damn, but the woman had him in knots. That wasn't a good thing either. He knew he had no business touching her. He should have subdued her last night when she'd come storming into his room and sent her back to the sanctuary of hers. But in the back of his mind, he knew if he'd found the will to do that, he'd have used the excuse of her having two beds in her room to sleep in there with her. Then he'd find his way into her bed anyway. He'd led her to believe he could sleep in there at any time to ensure her protection, but in the cold light of day, he knew if she was in that kind of danger, he wouldn't just want to sleep in the same room with her; he'd want her on the first flight out back to safety.

Because her life was suddenly too precious to chance.

Jesus, he was toast. He hadn't been in a relationship in years. Hadn't had the time for it. Hell, he didn't now. He was still in the military, didn't know how much longer he'd be in Afghanistan. She'd only be here another week or so. How was he supposed to build anything of substance with her? If they'd formed a relationship away from here before he'd been sent on this tour, maybe they could have made it work. His rotation allowed for ninety days of block leave. He could've wined and dined her over three months and built a strong foundation before being sent back overseas.

But it hadn't happened like that, and that bothered him. Not that he wasn't given the opportunity to build this up slowly. That didn't help matters, sure. It was the fact that they were in a warzone, brought together by chance, and could just as easily be ripped away from it.

Could it be considered *chance* if his sister was behind it?

Yes, yes, it could. Even *if* they could pick this thing building between them back up stateside after she left, he still had several months before he was eligible for discharge. Not that he'd decided if he was going to. The reality was, she would fly off into the sunset and he'd reenlist.

All logic screamed at him that touching her had been a mistake. There was no way this could be anything more than a temporary fling, but he knew if he continued to let himself steal away with her at night as he desperately wanted, and foster the intimate bond taking hold, he wouldn't be able to sit back and watch her walk away and out of his life when her project was over.

"I hear you've got a little problem on your hands."

Oh shit. Did this man know he'd crossed the erotic line last night? Crossed? Hell, he'd obliterated it over and over again.

"Seems your charge is a bit willful."

Axle scanned his memory and came smack face-to-face with the one where Caitlin had gotten out of his sight, and he'd glued himself to her hip.

"Why was she yelling at you, refusing your help in the helo?"

Fuck, he knew.

He could be vague and discuss Caitlin's combativeness in generalities, but Axle didn't want to paint her in a bad light, and it wasn't completely honest. She absolutely had a strong head on her shoulders, but it wasn't as if she hadn't been provoked. He'd kept the news of what happened between them last night to himself, but if he got asked outright, he'd have to own up to what happened and take the royal ass-chewing he'd get. Knowing he'd be upfront about the more intimate events of yesterday if asked told him there was no reason to hide exactly what had happened earlier in the day.

"Charlie walked away following a story lead while I was scanning the village perimeter. She did so without informing me or any member of my team of her intent. Similar to incident on her first venture out, she did not afford us the opportunity to clear the building she was near. She broke protocol, disobeyed orders, and I informed her I would no longer be outside of hand's reach of her. She did not take kindly to that, Sir."

Burge stared at him. If Axle wasn't so practiced with interrogation techniques, he'd have a bead of sweat on his forehead forming under the scrutiny. But he stood there completely calm and waiting for his commander's words.

"You lost sight of her."

Fuck.

"Yes."

For endless seconds, the man pinned him with his steely gaze. Then he rose slowly. "I think I didn't make myself clear when I put you on this assignment." He slammed his hands on his desk as he leaned closer.

Double fuck.

"Sir, my team had eyes on her the whole—"

"Except when she walked unescorted into an unsecured *goddamn* building days ago and attempted it again yesterday!"

"Yes, Sir." He couldn't say anything else. It was only seconds she was unattended, but he knew, in this world, it only took a split second for a sniper to drop a target or an

IED to detonate or an RPG to explode out of nowhere. They were at war. Plain and simple.

"You better pull your head outta your ass, Landry. No fucking mistakes. Do I make myself clear?"

"Yes, Sir!"

Burge took a deep breath and sat. "Sit down," he said, clearly still irritated. Axle did what he was told. "What's the status of her assignment?"

Axle blinked, unsure how to answer. "I don't know," he said slowly. "You ordered me to stay out of it. Not to discuss it. I'm protection only."

Burge cracked a smile. "Good answer." Whatever humor he'd felt quickly dissipated because his face turned steely. "I called you here because Asad Samim has been detained."

"What?" he asked slowly. The interpreter who'd been working with Caitlin had checked out, or so Axle had thought. "Why?" he snapped.

"The timing of the MOAB drop coincided with an arms delivery. Someone sold military grade weapons to ISIS. As you are aware, we put a stop to it."

"Yes, Sir." His SEAL Team had been briefed on the issue prior to scoping out the area. The air strike had been successful. The tunnels destroyed. The parties involved eliminated. Private William Adin Richardson had been captured and sent to a CIA black site for interrogation. "The defector has been detained, and Aarif Yasin KIA."

Burge gave him a sharp nod. "Asad Samim is his cousin."

The air left Axle's lung in a rush. Asad was Aarif's cousin? He'd been alone with Caitlin. A lot. If he'd wanted to kill her, he could have taken her out any number of times and there would've been nothing Axle could've done to save her. His jaw clenched. If that man touched one hair on her head... "He's a dead man."

"If it's all the same to you, we'd rather work him over until he spills everything," Burge drawled with a raised eyebrow.

"Yes, Sir." Axle fisted his hands in his lap to keep from breaking the first thing he could grab.

"I need you to encourage Ms. Cooper to finish her report and go back home. Richardson, Samim, Yasin, none of their names need to be leaked. Inform her Samim was discharged from duty for some minor infraction. We'll get her another interpreter. Unless the village attack is something bigger than initial appearance, you'll be free to fly in forty hours."

So, they wouldn't be able to fly tomorrow. He just hoped she didn't stay in her room all day since he wasn't sure if he'd be able to stick to his decision to keep things professional. He couldn't allow that.

"Can we enter the red zone via LUV? There are some nearby units we can travel to that were scheduled for next week. If I can move those up over the next two days and double up on flyovers once cleared, she could be finished within the week."

"That shouldn't be a problem. Anything else?"

"No, Sir." He was crystal clear on everything. Knowing he'd let a possible ISIS connection work closely with her only shored up his resolve, creating a solid steel cage around his chest and locking the reality into place. He had to protect her. That was it. And he had to double-time it on her agenda to get her out of his territory. He couldn't afford anymore distractions. Nada.

The best thing to do...the smart thing to do...was to nip what was happening between them in the bud. It'd be hard to do, but the more he thought about it, the more he knew it wasn't just *best* or *smart*, it was also the *right* thing to do. Whatever happened between them was over. End of fucking story.

"Dismissed."

Axle exited the building and called Acker as he hopped into the vehicle.

"Acker."

"We've been grounded for forty hours. I need to you pull the agenda, contact the COs of the last two units, and get them rescheduled the next two days."

"Yes, Sir."

Axle speed away. "In fact, we're going to move a lot of shit around. I want sixteen-hour days until she's on a C-130 back to the States. See what else you can get penciled in to shave off a few days from her trip."

"I'm on it, Sir."

"Where is she now?"

"She's with Lightweight in their regular meeting room."

He ended the communication and headed straight for where she was. His heart and his brain battled for supremacy, but the fact his heart was even in this competition showed him he'd made the right decision.

The thought of Lorenzo being close to her fueled more anger. Not only would he have to keep quiet as he watched the other man flirt shamelessly with her, he had to keep from beating the shit out of him for bringing Asad onto the assignment. Thankfully, by the time he arrived at the building, he'd leashed his fury, so that he could focus solely on Caitlin's protection. It was all that mattered now.

His team members snapped to attention when he walked into the room. "As you were," he muttered, his gaze on Caitlin.

Damn, she was beautiful. That luscious pink color highlighted her cheeks and grew darker as he looked at her. In the light of day, she was more breathtaking—no. He couldn't allow his thoughts to even wander to anything about her apart from his job.

"We're just getting ready to break, so I can change and prepare to do a live feed," she said excitedly.

"What's going on?"

"Lorenzo captured footage of some locals talking to men linked to the leader of ISIS and his top soldiers before they were killed."

Axle froze, but he hid any other reaction. "There were men linked to ISIS who were there while we were?" he asked, but he already knew that answer. The military wouldn't have detained Asad without reason. For all he knew, Asad had used the cover of his contracted job with the military to carry missives between Kabul and the villages near the border.

"Yeah, I need to freshen up before I report live." She was excited, and he had to fight the urge to smile and feel proud of her for coming across the information on her own. Of course, he'd have to stop her from learning more, and that was totally fucked up. It was one thing not to volunteer what he knew, but purposefully misleading her would be something altogether different. He shouldn't have to contemplate how to keep intel from her, but he had no choice. Guilt stabbed him. He possessed information that could skyrocket her career, but it was classified. His hands were tied. This story was DOA and there wasn't a damn thing he could do to let her know.

She walked toward the door and he followed her out, tamping down all the warring urges within. He wanted her, but he couldn't have her. He wanted to help her, but it was his career and his freedom if he did. He was well and truly fucked no matter how he looked at it. He had to talk to her, but he wasn't sure how he would find the words that wouldn't hurt him *and* her when he expressed them. The one thing he did know for sure in all this was that dreaded conversation had to take place. No matter how hard it would be, he'd have to do it anyway.

The sooner the better.

When they arrived at the barracks, he told Brooks to stay back and keep watch while he followed her inside. She reached her door, and he stood at the threshold as she walked in. She turned to shut the door, but he clamped his hand on it to stop her.

She grinned, her gaze darting past him before meeting his again. "I have to change. I don't want to do it where anybody can walk in and see." Then her smile turned sultry. "If you behave, you can watch."

Jesus. Soon was looking like *now* because he wanted to nod like a fool and throw everything away. The temptation was almost unbearable. The only thing stronger than his desire for her was his resolve—for her. If it wasn't sad, he'd laugh at how one woman could push and pull him from multiple directions all at the same time.

Doesn't matter. Be direct. He knew how to steel himself and deal with all kinds of shitty situations. He could do this. He would.

"I can't stay. I just wanted to tell you what happened last night can't happen again."

Her smile faltered until her mouth hung open.

"It was great. You were great. It's just not smart. I have a job to do, and I fucked up by letting my cock do the thinking. It won't happen again."

She still didn't say anything, and her eyes turned glassy.

He cussed and turned, shutting the door behind him, needing that barrier between them to keep from pulling her into his arms and telling her to forget what he just said. That he'd been wrong.

He wasn't wrong, though, and that was what tore him up the most.

CHAPTER TWELVE

CAITLIN HIT the alarm before it had a chance to go off. She'd been awake for hours, dreading another heartless day in the dessert.

It'd been several days since she'd come across a piece of news that had her squealing and her boss salivating. She'd been eager to share it with Axle, but he'd pulled the rug out from under her, shutting her out without warning. He told her what happened that night between them—and all the moments leading up to it—had been a mistake. She'd been blindsided. She hadn't known it was possible to have the wind knocked out of her without physically being punched. She now knew the truth. He'd dealt that emotional blow, and she'd almost cried right there in front of him. She'd beat back the tears of shock stinging her eyes, demanding to form and fall, so she'd been grateful he'd left when he had. She was already embarrassed enough without suffering even more humiliation of traitor tears.

She hadn't the time to wrap her head around it either, because she had a live feed immediately following. Her report couldn't wait, and television wouldn't have cared her heart was breaking.

Because it had been.

It still was, opening her eyes to another devastating revelation. She'd fallen in love with him, a man who didn't want her. The realization slammed into her, crushing her delicate heart all over again.

She didn't know how she could fall in love as fast as she had. She'd heard of people meeting and marrying from whirlwind romances, but she'd assumed those people had been blinded with lust on their road to love. It had just seemed implausible to her. Now, she knew the all-consuming truth. It wasn't only a possibility. It was her reality. If she hadn't met Axle, she'd still believe falling in love so quickly was impossible. She knew with painful clarity now that she'd been so terribly, utterly wrong. There was zero doubt in her mind and her heart how she felt. But she also understood that, unlike those blindly fast courtships, there would be no happily ever after for them.

Something else she'd had trouble reconciling was his own conflicting behavior. Oh, he hadn't said anything to her to make her think he'd second-guessed his decision. Since crushing her world, Axle had been emotionally distant as one might expect, but he'd hovered around as if he was ready to take a bullet for her. It seemed he cared more than he wanted. She reminded herself time and time again he was just doing his job, but the conflicting emotions rolling off him confused her.

And infuriated her.

He seemed to master being right there without being there at all. He talked to her only when he had to, and even then it was all business. He hadn't touched her since that night either. Not a hand on her elbow to guide her somewhere, nothing. Not that there hadn't been opportunity. Since the morning after their night of passion, he'd worked them all to the bone. Before sunup to way past sundown. He'd managed to reschedule a bunch of excursions, cramming them together and knocking off days from her original itinerary. He'd been a machine, seeming to need not food, water, or even rest. He was focused, and she hated the real reason for it.

He was determined to get her the heck away from him.

Yeah, that burned.

She couldn't do it again today, and she knew that was exactly what would happen if she got out of this bed and carried on like nothing had happened. She couldn't deal with him anymore, not that he'd dealt with her much. Alec had brought her meals ever since Axle's curt words, and she'd been relieved—and hurt. Every night, she'd wanted to stay in the hallow protection of her room, but if she hadn't walked down the short hall to shower, she would've had to do a sponge bath in her sink. She was pitiful enough to admit to herself today that she'd seriously considered that as an option the last couple of nights. The shower had eventually won out, enticing her with the possibility of feeling even marginally better. It hadn't worked, and each morning had been more difficult than the last. Now, she was emotionally and physically exhausted. She needed a break from Axle, from the heartache, and she damn well deserved it.

What could he do if she refused to leave the barracks? Carry her, kicking and screaming, onto a helicopter or into one of those military vehicles? He'd have to actually touch her to do that. Yeah, that wasn't happening. He'd proved that days ago.

A knock sounded on her door.

"Go away," she muttered, but she'd said it loud enough for the person to hear.

She heard some shuffling in the hallway. The guy was probably just making sure she hadn't overslept. She'd been taking showers in the evening because she hadn't wanted to go to sleep all gritty, and she liked sleeping in as long as possible. It wouldn't take them long to figure out she wasn't stepping foot outside the barracks today.

She sat up and grabbed her laptop. There weren't any emails from her producer, but Lorenzo had uploaded some more footage. He hadn't been chatty lately, almost having taken a personal offense to the translator being replaced. Axle hadn't explained why, and she hadn't been in the frame of mind to ask. Lorenzo had cussed and demanded answers, though. She knew the two of them had worked together in the past, so she did feel bad for Lorenzo in that respect. She could spend the day playing catch-up on what was captured the last few days and reach out to him if she had any questions.

So it wasn't as if staying in today meant she wouldn't be working. There was plenty she could do.

She'd spent about fifteen minutes watching the same part over and over again. She needed the translator watch it, too, so she'd know what some of the people in the background were saying. It could be nothing, but she didn't want to miss anything. She was still concentrating on the section when another knock landed on her door.

"I said. Go. Away," she said slowly, but louder this time.

More footsteps sounded. One of the poor guys was probably about to get their butt chewed for not following orders to keep her on schedule. She'd apologize to whoever it was later. In fact, she needed to get contact information on all the men on her protection team, so she could send them care packages when she returned home. None of them asked to be on this assignment, so it was the least she could do to show her appreciation. For now, though, she was taking this time for herself.

Knock. Knock. Knock. "Ms. Cooper, transports are loaded. We secured chow for you." Whoever it was sounded a little nervous.

"I have other stuff to do today."

She started another clip.

Someone else stepped up to the door. "Caitlin, this is Brooks."

"Hey, Brooks," she called back to him. "I tried to explain to the other guy that I'm not going today."

"Um—"

"Please relay that info to all parties. Thanks."

"O-okay." Yeah, she definitely needed to do something nice for them all.

Realizing she'd watched this particular footage already, she fast-forwarded the video, but she didn't get far before having to pause it. Someone had slammed the main door and was now stomping toward her room. She didn't have to hear his voice to know who was going to be on the other side any second now.

Bang. Bang. Bang. Bang. Bang. "Caitlin," Axle said tersely. "The demilitarization zone is ninety-seven klicks. We need to un-ass now to keep schedule."

"I told Brooks and whoever else knocked that I'm not going. You can reschedule it."

The knob rattled right before her door flew open, but she gasped anyway when it hit the wall. She should've known Axle would come barging in.

She tore her gaze away from him and tried to act

nonchalant. "Good morning," she said as she went back to watching the video.

"You're not dressed," he said, and she hated the fact that he'd voiced it so cold.

"Depends on your definition." She'd slept in a tank and shorts because she if she had to exit the building quickly in the middle of the night, she didn't want to be in a t-shirt and panties.

"We don't have time for games, Caitlin. You need to put your ass in gear and get some clothes on."

She turned up the volume on her laptop in an effort to show him she was seriously not going anywhere. Although she didn't look at him now, she could feel his anger building. She didn't have to see his face to see the vein in his forehead bulging.

"Seems I missed my calling," Alec said when he walked in with a tray of food. He put it on her bedside table along with a cup of coffee. "I wonder if waiters get hazard pay."

"Oh, thank you." She smiled and reached for the dark, steaming liquid.

"Wait outside," Axle said, and she knew he wasn't talking to her. "We'll be out in a minute."

She looked at him then as the guys started to file out. "I know you understand English. I'm not going. Get. Out."

The men crowding her door froze, obviously shocked at the way she'd talked to their leader, and he barked, "Now." They scrambled to leave, and Axle shut the door behind them. When he turned to look at her, her gaze shot to her laptop, pretending to be deep in work.

The seconds ticked by.

He took a step toward her, and her heart leapt. She hated having that reaction. Hated it. Hopefully, it was just adrenaline from the confrontation and not because this was first time they'd been alone since he threw up his emotional barriers.

The room was so tiny, but with him in it, she felt claustrophobic. He filled the space with just his presence, but his size was commanding it, too, consuming every void. He took another step and sat on the other bed in the room.

He was as far from her as possible in this little space, but he could stretch his arm out and graze her.

He wouldn't, though. She knew he wouldn't dare.

God, I hope he doesn't.

That was a lie. She wanted him to touch her, hold her, kiss her...

"What's wrong?" he asked almost softly.

She gaped at him. "Are you fucking joking?"

He nodded slowly. "So this is about us?"

"There is no us. You made that painfully clear." Her eyes stung, so she quickly looked away to get her bearings. She shook her head infinitesimally as she grappled with herself not to show any emotion. She couldn't show any weakness. She'd already lost, but he didn't have to know that.

Her bed dipped, and her gaze flew in that direction even though she knew the reason.

Axle. He'd sat on her bed. If he was all-consuming in the other corner, he was downright lethal this close to her. Not to her life, no. She'd never think that of him. But he was to her heart, her head. To everything else that mattered.

He searched her eyes, his darting back and forth between hers. He finally said, "I can't decide if I want to kill my sister for getting me involved with this or thank her."

She frowned at him, not sure what he meant and also partly surprised he was talking to her about something personal. He'd been strictly business now for several days. "What are you talking about?"

"That this is such a small world." He shrugged and looked ahead, but not really looking at anything in particular. "You mentioned Ishmael is the reason you have protection, but why me? Why not someone else? Someone more involved with frontline work might've been a better fit, or at least a more seamless one. God knows, there are qualified men stationed here that could've taken this duty." He hesitated, but she was almost too scared to speak for fear he'd clam up. He looked at her again. "My sister, that's why. She works with him. Your friend."

"Oh." She'd wondered before if Axle worked with Hunter. When she'd called her childhood friend and he'd dismissed the notion that Axle was a mercenary, she hadn't though much else about it. She'd assumed Axle had been randomly selected for this operation when Hunter hadn't known him. "When did you figure it out?"

"When she told me about Ishmael."

"So she knows him," she said, letting the news settle as she moved her laptop aside. It was possible his sister worked with him and didn't really know him. Caitlin worked with a lot of people she didn't personally know, but there had to be a relationship of some kind for his sister to help Hunter pull the strings.

"Ishmael? No. But Hunter Anderson?" he asked, tilting his head to the side as if catching her in the lie.

Caitlin winced playfully. "Technically, his name isn't Hunter anyway."

"I know. Had some sleepless nights I needed to somehow fill. Digging up intel on your boyfriend back home seemed like a wonderful way to torture myself."

She didn't know what to say about that. Hunter never

was and never would be her boyfriend. Plus, there was the whole looking-into-her-causing-him-pain aspect of that statement. Instead, she asked, "What does your sister do?"

Just because Axle wasn't a mercenary didn't mean his sister wasn't. She didn't think it was common for women to be involved in that life, but anything was possible.

"Not an easy question to answer," he said slowly.

"Does it have anything to do with being paid to handle problems?"

He frowned. Opened his mouth. Closed it. He shook his head. "She's not a psychologist, if that's what you mean. I'm not exactly sure what she is right now. Something happened, and she's going through some, I don't know, *regret* maybe, with the path she chose."

"Ahh." *Because she's a mercenary.*

"Shit went south on her last assignment. Somebody betrayed her team, and she got shot."

"Wow, she's okay, though, right?"

"Mm-hmm. Just thinking if she wants to live the dangerous life."

Oh yeah, she's definitely mercenary.

"I take it her career choice didn't sit well with you?" He was a regimented military man, and what his sister did was illegal.

He laughed lightly. "Hell no. Dad and I gave her a lot of shit about it."

Caitlin gaped at him. "She told your parents? I'd think that would be something you couldn't tell everybody about." She wasn't sure how long Heather knew about Hunter, but her friend had kept it from her even after drunken nights in Vegas.

"I—er, what do you think she does?"

Caitlin grimaced. "You know...takes care of problems... for cash."

He smiled. "I'mma need you to be more direct than that."

The way he looked at her had her second-guessing her theory. If she wasn't a mercenary, then why was she working with Hunter? She could be a mechanic. Axle had told her about his father's garage back home. She could be working with Hunter in that respect.

Working under cars could be dangerous, but that wouldn't explain why she'd been shot. "Do you know what Hunter does?"

His gaze narrowed. "I know it had to be illegal on some level to get the feds involved."

"But your sister knows?"

"Yeah. She's an FBI agent assigned to work their case, or contract, or whatever the hell it is."

"Ohh." Okay, that made sense. "I thought she was one of *his* teammates." Then she laughed. "You know, because of the betrayal and shooting and working for money."

He seemed to contemplate that, and she worried she'd said more than she should have. She didn't know much about Hunter's team and had every intention of getting more information from Heather when she got back, but it seemed Axle knew even less. "No," he said with a pause. "She's a linguistics expert. Speaks half a dozen languages."

"Really?" she asked, genuinely intrigued and a little relieved he didn't ask more about Hunter.

"Yeah. Smart as shit. Doesn't always get to focus on translations," he said with an eyeroll.

"Uh-oh," she said jokingly. "I don't think I should ask about that."

He chuckled. "Best not to. It involves a questionable sexual harassment thing."

She curled her lip. "Most women have those."

"What happened to you?" he asked. She didn't really want to get into it, but the tone of his question told her he wasn't going to let her get away without answering.

"Nothing major. Just a slimy experience with the now lieutenant governor of Arkansas."

"Hmm," he said, almost as if filing away that information.

"Don't suppose your sister speaks Pashto," she said offhandedly, partly as a distraction.

"I'm not sure." He shrugged. "I know she studied Arabic and a host of Middle Eastern dialects. The feds pay big money for language skills even if linguistics isn't someone's primary focus."

"You think she'd mind watching some videos and listening to people speaking in the background?" she asked without thinking. "Sorry, she's probably busy working on a case or something. Forget I asked." She waved her hand and looked away from him. It was too easy to talk.

To forget.

She missed this, speaking freely with him.

She missed him.

"I'll ask her," he said gently.

She nodded and glanced at him. "Why didn't you tell me before that she got you involved in this?"

He raised an eyebrow. "Engaging in causal conversation wasn't high up on my priority list the night she told me. There were other, more intimate activities that demanded my focus."

Caitlin felt her face flame, and she watched as his breathing got deeper, almost labored.

"You are so beautiful when you do that," he whispered so lightly that she almost missed hearing it. It felt like a confession to her alone that no one else could ever hear.

Her body rioted with her brain. She wanted to reach out to him, but he stayed locked in place. His words had come from the heart, but she could tell they wouldn't change anything. In that moment, though, she began to understand. He hadn't wanted to stop what was happening. Not completely. Something or someone had made that decision. Even if that person was himself, she could see it hadn't been as cut and dried for him as she'd assumed.

"I can't help it," she murmured, not really sure how to proceed around the elephant in this tiny space with them. "Happens when I get embarrassed or uncomfortable or—"

"Turned on," he said, interrupting her. "Come so hard your whole body shakes. I know. Fuck, I know." His head lowered slightly, but his gaze never wavered. Her palms began to sweat as the moisture in her mouth completely dissipated at his voiced memory. Of her. Of them. "I know exactly where that red tint spreads on your body," he said, his voice raspy.

"Axle," she breathed.

He shut his eyes on a sigh. "I'm sorry. I don't know what it is about you, but I can't do this." He shook his head and looked at her again. Even though his words were no different than the before, where last time he'd spoken them with cold finality, this time, his torment shone through. Her heart wanted to comfort him. To tell him it'd be okay. Her brain saw it for the lie it was. Words used to soothe, to excuse just one more touch. She couldn't do that to herself. It would only cause more pain.

Her body didn't get the message. Before she registered her movement, she reached for him. His hand shot out and fisted her hair, stopping her advancement. She'd grabbed his arm on instinct, not to pull him away, but to stabilize herself. His wild gaze pinned her for the briefest of moments, but it felt like a dozen lifetimes passed as he stared at her, into her soul, neither moving, both held prisoner as time seemed to stand still.

"Please," she breathed. If this was goodbye, she at least wanted a kiss to remember him. She needed it more than her next breath. It would help her accept the fact that she had to let him go.

That was a lie, too. She still didn't care. She'd learn to deal with the pain later because no matter what, when they went their separate ways, there would be crushing hurt.

There would be no getting over this man.

He groaned before leaning toward her while tugging her toward him. Blood rushed in her veins in anticipation. He was going to kiss her. One last time. The moment his lips brushed against hers, she let go of his forearm and, with shaking hands, skimmed up his biceps to cup his neck. She let out a moan when his tongue slipped into her mouth, and that broke whatever tether was holding him back. His other hand dove into her hair, clutching her to him as he deepened the kiss. It was powerful and passionate.

Tender and sad.

Her breath caught just as he pulled away. He kissed her cheek twice and her forehead once before letting go of her and standing.

"I can push back this morning's stop, shorten the time we spend at both locations, and we can get back late tonight." His mouth was still red, lips swollen. She wiped her own as she watched him. His eyes dilated, but that was the only reaction.

"I can be ready in three minutes." She'd be dead on her

feet, but it'd be the right thing to do. The faster she finished her story, the quicker she could leave. If anything could help, it'd be distance. Besides, if she didn't keep today's itinerary, others would be inconvenienced. She honestly didn't want that to happen.

He nodded once. "Send me whatever video you want me to have my sister watch. Can't promise Shelby will be able to help, but she can take a look."

"Thanks," she said, hoping her voice didn't crack too much.

Then he indicated the tray of food on the table beside her bed. "Grab that, too. You can eat in the transport."

She took a fortifying breath and saluted. "Sir, yes, Sir," she said without the urgency of anybody else she'd heard giving the command.

He cracked a smile. "I'll be waiting for you," he said before walking out.

"If only that was true," she whispered to the closed door.

"DO you have any idea how early it is?" Shelby asked Axle when she answered his call.

Any hope of finishing early today crashed and burned the moment they'd gotten a late start. Caitlin had refused to leave at first, and he'd been ready to pull her over his lap and spank her ass. Yeah, it was barbaric, but the image taunted him as he griped at her about holding them up. She'd eventually agreed to continue on as scheduled, and it had taken every ounce of strength not to cancel everything anyway and spend the day locked in her room showing just how bossy he could be.

"Sorry, Sis. Couldn't be helped."

"You look like dog doo."

He exhaled a short chuckle. "Feel like it too."

"At least you showered, or you'd smell like it too, I bet."

"No doubt." A cold shower had cleaned the grime and helped wake him up enough to call a couple of his teammates and his sister. He talked to the guys first, knowing those conversations would be short, and hoped the one with Shelby would be too. He was tuckered out. Looking out his open doorway to Caitlin's closed door, he asked, "Did ya get the link I sent to the video library? They were too large to attach to an email."

"Yep. Most of what I heard seemed irrelevant—talking about markets and wives and such—but there were two different conversations that contained interesting details. One talked about the MOAB, referring to it as Mother. There's mention of U.S. Military involvement in an arms deal."

"Shit," he breathed.

"What?" she asked slowly.

He sighed. "It classified. I can't go into it."

"Dude, then why would you ask me to translate it for a *journalist*?"

"Fuck, I don't know." He rubbed his head. "She needed help with the footage. How was I supposed to know some random villagers would be discussing it?"

"Um, because she was there reporting on it?" she asked sarcastically. "People aren't stupid."

"Apparently, I am. Fuck." He looked at the ceiling, trying to figure out what to do now. "What all was said?"

"The gist? Some soldiers were there, asking about selling weapons, and days later, the good ol' boys came back with bombs to cover their tracks."

"Jesus Christ. That's not how it went down."

"Were there traitors selling arms?"

"I can't answer that."

"That's a yes. Is that where the explosion was?"

He groaned.

"That's another yes. Doesn't matter if that's not *why* forces dropped the bomb. The locals believe that, and a journalist has every right to report local reactions to what's going on in their town."

"I'll tell her you couldn't help."

"Too late. I've already noted the timestamp and sent a transcript to the email address on the video library link."

A litany of cusswords flew from his mouth.

"What's the problem here?" she asked. "I mean, I get what really happened is classified information, but it's not like somebody with the inside scoop told her anything."

"I was *ordered* not to help her with her research."

"Yeah, but you didn't. I did." She shrugged.

"Burge is not going to see it that way." Axle wouldn't either if the shoe was on the other foot. "Shit's going to hit the fan when news comes out."

"Hate to break it to you, big brother, but there's another conversation on one of the clips that's much more damning."

He stared at her, hoping she was not about to tell him about the tunnels they'd destroyed. It'd been a major hub for the Taliban, and the government did not want that information known to the general public. They'd been used for more than illegal weapons purchases. "What did you hear?"

"Not just me. It was hard to make out, so I asked Viola to watch."

"You showed it to a federal agent?" he asked incredulously.

"She's my friend," Shelby defended. "She couldn't make out anything, either, but she did suggest I have Gauge enhance the audio."

"Who's that?" he asked, but deep down, he knew, and it was bad. "Tell me you did not send the video to the FBI."

"No, not technically. I mean, yeah, Gauge was an agent, but he works for the Bang Shift now, which means he's teammates with Hunter." She hesitated while his brain continued to spin. "I was surprised she even mentioned him," she said quickly. "She and Gauge have a history, and she usually avoids anything to do with him. When she said he should take a look, I about crapped my—"

"Shelby! What the fuck is going on?"

"Jeez. There was background noise that made it difficult for me to understand the conversation these two men were having. Gauge did some computer magic and cleared it. Meaning, he knows about its existence, but I didn't tell him what I translated."

"Good."

"Yet," Shelby added.

"What the hell does that mean?"

"Someone needs to know about it. I haven't decided who'd be best to get this information. If I wasn't on leave, I'd tell Rick and let him figure out how to address it, but since Gauge helped, I don't know. His team takes contracts to handle messes the government doesn't want to be connected to. This has the makings of being a huge government FUBAR, as you'd say, so I thought maybe the Bang Shift could deal with it."

Fucked up beyond all repair. The motto of this mission. "Deal with what?" he asked slowly.

"It's bigger than them, though. This could have far reaching implications."

"Goddamn it, Shelby…"

"The two guys were talking about prices being put on U.S. military targets. *People,* Axle."

He frowned at her. "It's well-known we all have a price on our head over here. This is war, and the Taliban pays good money the higher the rank of the target."

"I understand that, but where does the Taliban get the money? Seems they're more focused on spending their funds on weapons to fight their guerrilla-warfare-style battles, right?"

"True. And if Caitlin's story wasn't focused on that angle, it sure will once she reads your email." He glared at her, still needing to figure out what he was going to do about that.

"Sorry, Bub. You asked me to translate it." She shrugged. "But her story will be more explosive than the bomb itself. Those two men weren't just talking about how much money they could make taking out members of U.S. forces and its allies. They mentioned where the terrorists got the money to fund the rewards."

"Jesus, we have more traitors in the midst." It was the only explanation. The U.S. had tons of money to blow on the war effort and thousands of smart people with varying levels of intel. Money made people do stupid things.

Private William Adin Richardson had already proven that by selling weapons to the enemy.

"The money didn't come from the U.S. It came from Russia."

"What?" he asked, drawing out the word.

"I don't know. Their conversation was short, but there's no doubt Russia is funding the rewards on the deaths of American and Allied fighters."

"Holy shit." Shelby was right. This was huge. Russia

was a world superpower, just like the U.S. If they were covertly taking out Americans through the guise of the Taliban...

"Exactly. So you see why I feel like I need to let someone know *before* this hits the press."

"What makes you think they don't?" he asked, being realistic. They had ears on all kinds of communication. Chances were, if locals were openly talking about it, the U.S. government already knew. If that was the case, Caitlin had stumbled upon classified information that was above his paygrade.

Caitlin's door opened across the hall, and his gaze darted toward it.

She walked into his room. Even still dirty, she was the most beautiful creature to him. She hadn't stormed in like before, and he stayed still, waiting, partly transfixed by her, but also wanting to see what she was going to do...to say. Had she read the emails from his sister? Had she come in to confront him with the truth?

Had she come to him for other reasons?

"What're you looking at?" his sister asked, but he didn't dare take his eyes off Caitlin.

She then tossed something at him, and he didn't have to look at it to know what it was.

His pen.

Without a word, she walked out, went back into her room, and closed the door. He'd kept his door open to keep watch of her room, but there was a sadistic part of him that didn't want to block any glimpse of her he could get. He knew those opportunities were numbered, and like an addict, he needed his fix no matter what it cost him in the end.

"Ax?"

He shut his eyes and took a deep breath. "What?"

"Is someone in there?"

"Not anymore."

"Who—"

"Caitlin," he said, penning his sister with a *fuck you* look.

"Uh-oh."

"Don't start with me."

"Damn, you have it bad for her."

"I'm not talking about this with you."

"Okay," she said slowly. "But have you talked about it with yourself? Because you didn't see your eyes just then."

"Shelby. Don't. For real. I can't go there with you. I'm fucking serious."

She nodded slowly. "All right, but I think there's something you should know."

He shook his head, ready for this conversation to be over. "If you tell me Ishmael is in love with her, you do realize I will fucking kill him, don't you?"

"No way. Dude is totally head over heels for his girlfriend, who, by the way, I hear is behind the Ishmael profile name. Get it? *Moby Dick*. He probably has a huge—"

"Jesus Christ. You can't focus for five seconds. How in the world did you ever learn a bunch of languages?" he asked, exasperated.

"Ha. Ha," she said, deadpan. "But this isn't about Hunter. It's about Gauge. The more I thought about it, the more I thought it was weird Viola had suggested him to enhance the video. There are other computer experts whose connection to the bureau isn't as hazy."

"Maybe she understood you looking at the footage needed to stay secret. You said he wasn't technically a fed anymore."

"Yeah, that was my thought, too."

"But," he said, waving his hand, encouraging her to continue.

"But, remember, when I mentioned you being assigned to Caitlin that *he* was the one who was the driving force behind it? When I backpedaled on suggesting to do it, he argued you were the best choice. He made the calls. *He* made it happen."

"Uh-huh. You said that before."

"Well, you're never in a million years going to believe who he is."

CHAPTER THIRTEEN

DEAD ON HER FEET, that was the only way to describe how Caitlin felt. Her fit yesterday morning hadn't backed them up too much on their schedule, but it had caused a domino effect. Twenty-five minutes late leaving, being rerouted in transit, forty minutes extra at first location, it all added up. By the time they'd gotten back last night, it was late enough for her to video call her producer and not be too early for him to answer. She'd gathered enough footage that she was free to wrap up her investigation and head back at the end of the week. She should've been happy to hear that. With the hours she'd put in on the last several assignments, she was due a vacation.

Somewhere not hot and dirty, and preferably not hazardous to her life and wellbeing.

No weapons of mass destruction.

No rocky terrain.

No testosterone-filled groups.

It wasn't only because of Axle why she sought a man-free refuge. The men on his team had all taken a turn hovering around her at one point or another, and when she'd eventually come out of the barracks yesterday morning, each of them had ragged her. She'd shown her ass, not wanting to leave, and ten minutes alone with their commander, and she was hightailing out of her room.

They didn't know the two of them had been locking lips. As far they figured, he'd chewed her ass out, and she'd jumped to comply. She hadn't been able to correct their thinking. No, she'd had to take the ribbing in stride. It would've been easier if Axle had put a stop to it, but that would've looked suspicious and brought on scrutiny he hadn't wanted. By the time they'd reached the first stop, the comments from them had died down, and she'd been able to put all of her focus onto work.

Okay, *most* of her focus. She still watched Axle. He'd kept his word and stayed far enough away so that he didn't interfere with her interviews, but he'd never taken his eyes off her. Each time she looked at him, he met her gaze, and she'd always been the first one to look away. It frustrated her that he'd been so close but so far. It pleased her to know he cared enough to not lose sight of her. It saddened her to know their time was limited.

She'd gone through a complete range of emotions throughout the day and into the night back at the barracks. Even when getting ready for her shower, she'd berated herself for all the conflicting emotions coursing through her. As she'd gathered her toiletries and metaphorical big girl panties, she'd caught sight of Axle's note and pen from the side of her bag, taunting her all over again. She'd been on the frustration cycle at that moment, so she'd dropped her shower supplies and grabbed the piece of paper he'd left for her the morning after their night of passion. Without hesitation, she'd ripped the note into shreds.

It hadn't been as satisfying as she'd hoped. She

should've known better, but logic had no place among the vast feelings she'd been experiencing.

She'd picked up the pen and looked at it. It'd crossed her mind to have it meet the same fate as the note, but she didn't think it'd destroy easily. Apparently, she'd possessed a tiny bit of sense after all.

Not enough, though. She was hurt, not crazy. Besides, it didn't belong to her anyway. Breaking it might've given her momentary satisfaction, but it wouldn't last, and then she'd feel guilty. She couldn't in good conscience break something that wasn't hers, but neither could she keep it around. It belonged to Axle.

So she'd done the only thing she could.

When she'd walked out of her room, his door was open, and Axle spied her from his perch on his bed.

The one they'd shared.

The last time she'd gone in there with that pen, she'd been furious and had hurled at it him, hoping to cause harm. What had transpired had hurt her more in the end than any damage she could have done to him in that moment in time.

Rather than storm in with fury nipping at her heels, she'd wordlessly stepped into his room and tossed it gently with perfect aim onto his bed. It had landed by his feet and bounced by his boot. Her gazed had stayed locked on his until it came to a stop. With the note tattered and the pen returned, she'd have no more reminders of him in the sanctuary of her room.

It was as it should've been.

She'd returned to gather the rest of her toiletries and retreated to the shower. A large part of her hoped he'd follow her in there—a part she'd wanted to smack.

He never did. The man was keeping his distance.

When she'd finished, she'd gone back to her room without looking through his open doorway. It had been tough, but she'd found the will somehow.

She'd left her laptop and had intended on glancing at her messages before turning her lights out and going to sleep.

What she saw jolted her awake.

Shelby Landry had messaged her.

And blown her story wide open.

Caitlin had spent the next couple of hours gathering her notes for her next live report. She wanted to make sure she had all of the angles covered for what would be the shocking newsbreak of her career.

This morning, nothing had changed with Axle, but her mind was reeling. How much had he known? Had it played a part at all in him pushing her away? She wanted to ask him, but she couldn't risk him stopping her live segment.

But if his sister had sent her the information, she could have also sent it to him. The desire to talk to him about the U.S. arms deals and Russia's funding of the Taliban were great, but she bit her tongue, hoping he'd show his hand first.

He hadn't. He'd been just as distant with her as before.

Maybe even more so.

When they'd boarded the helicopter earlier, he hadn't helped her strap in, though he'd stood in front of her staring down, watching as she secured the harness. She mentally jumped from wanting to demand he acknowledge what was happening...either in this country or between them, she wasn't sure.

Had he seen her as nothing more than a fling? Would he deny his feelings if she pressed him?

Would he tell her if she asked him outright about his mission and the rewards the Russians were offering?

She wanted all the answers, but she was scared of the truth. She bet Christiane Amanpour never had that problem.

Caitlin battled with wanting to force him to deny what they both knew was true and face it head on together while also wanting to catch the first flight out of this country and forget she ever met him.

She was so confused, but she knew once she was gone, she'd never feel his gaze on her again and that had scared her on a completely different level.

If the previous few days had been torture, the last twenty-four hours had been a new agony.

At least focusing on work helped dull the ache a little. She was in the middle of an interview with the sixth villager who'd agreed to speak to her in yet another part of the Achin District. No new information had developed from direct sources since they'd been farther east a couple of days ago, but several had confirmed what she'd learned, which was also important.

She asked a question, and Karzai, the interpreter who'd replaced Asad, translated her question. Her new colleague wasn't as relaxed as Asad had been. Where this guy was laser focused, Asad had been laidback. Karzai had done an excellent job, though, always quick to relay her questions and speak the responses clearly. She'd been impressed with him, but honestly, she'd been with Asad too. Being able to speak a second language took an extraordinary amount of discipline.

She could only imagine the dedication it took for Axle's sister to learn several.

. . .

WHEN HE TOLD her flatly that Asad had been removed from duty without any other explanation, she hadn't thought much about it. The locals ironically had a freedom the military force did not. They could come and go as they wanted. Some earned enough to care for their families for months with these assignments and would worry about money later when they ran low again.

It was no wonder there was a certain number who sought out the rewards that came at the cost of human lives. She understood some had a hatred toward Americans and probably saw it as a bonus to kill those they'd happily do away with anyway. They were at war, after all, and the reality was a frightening one. Thankfully, most of these people just wanted their home back from any strict Taliban control and understood the need of foreign help to make it happen. They didn't necessarily like it, but a necessary evil of sorts to achieve what they ultimately wanted.

"Stand on this side," Lorenzo barked at her. "There's a glare from the sun."

Although she'd had no reason to question Axle about Asad's replacement, Lorenzo had been the complete opposite. He'd demanded answers, reiterating that he'd worked with Asad for years, but Axle had shut down his questions that morning, ushering them to the helicopter to load up and head out. Ever since that day, Lorenzo had been a bear with a sore paw, either outright ignoring her questions about the footage or snapping at her about the camera angles and the questions she'd been asking the locals.

He'd been pissed and had taken it out on her. He was smart enough not to anger the troops because, if he irritated them, he'd be gone just as fast as Asad. Not that she was pleased with his tone. If she hadn't been so consumed with Axle, she might've taken him to task sooner, called him out on his attitude toward her, but she had more important things to focus on. She just bit her tongue and did what he asked, like right now, moving over so he could get a better shot as he finished setting up the still camera for the live feed.

In just a few minutes, this story would be all over the world.

She turned back to the man she'd been interviewing, knowing she only had time for a few more questions before her segment began.

"Sir, do you know anything about the alleged member of the Shinwari tribe recruited by ISIS?" she asked directly, and Karzai translated her question.

The villager quickly answered, and Karzai repeated in English, "Yes. His name was Aarif Yasin. He was killed when the bomb dropped."

She blinked, his answer rolling around in her head, slowing clicking together with what she'd learned last night. "Wait a minute. Are you telling me the U.S. dropped a bomb targeting tunnels and just so happened to take out a man who'd been buying weapons from the military?"

Karzai asked her question, but she didn't need to hear the translated confirmation to understand his answer. It was exactly what he was saying. There was more to his answer, though, that she needed repeated in English.

She glanced at Lorenzo, and he had a blank look in his eyes. The camera he held to do split screen live footage drooped slightly as he stared at Karzai, waiting for the translation. She turned her focus back to him.

"Yes. The American known to them only as *War* had been scheduled to meet with Aarif Yasin the day of the air strike. The tunnel was supposed to be inspected as a possible means for moving the merchandise undetected."

Lorenzo cussed, dropping his camera completely before walking away. "Hey," she called after him. Where was he going? This was important information. It clearly backed up Shelby's notes from last night, informing her Americans had sold weapons to the Taliban. There hadn't been a name mentioned on the footage Shelby had translated for her.

What if the military had dropped the MOAB to take out one man specifically? She'd already started to believe the bombing might not have only been about the tunnels before she'd arrived here. She'd been tasked to find the story, and she had.

A big one.

Who was this man the military cared so much about? And who was the War man? Had he been taken out, too, or maybe even the target? Her mind was racing through all these questions, her journalistic instincts screaming she needed that name. Had the military learned one of their own was trafficking arms and tried to cover this up? Running guns was bad enough, but if a ranked officer was behind it, that was crimes-against-country serious and could potentially implicate a lot of people.

Or he could've been a Russian, which opened up another can of worms.

Either way, this story could be huge.

The story of her *career*.

It didn't even register at that moment if she'd tapped into something major, she'd be here a lot longer, digging into it, but she was too excited to think beyond this minute. She needed to record this source for her producer.

"Lorenzo!"

He turned around and yelled, "Going to record the roadblock." He walked faster across the dusty street.

"I need you here!"

Her earpiece crackled.

"Caitlin, can you hear me?" Jack, her producer, asked.

"Yeah, I got you, Jack."

"Good. We're rolling. I'll count you in in approximately sixty seconds."

"I'll be ready."

Axle had been standing across the small street off camera, but jogged the few paces in her direction when she'd yelled after her retreating cameraman. "What's going on?"

"Not sure. I wanted him to record this interview, but my producer just told me we're recording now. I'll just keep asking this guy questions, and it should be captured by the main camera. It's fine."

"Okay," Axle said, and, by his tone, he didn't completely believe her. He stepped to the side, but staying closer than he'd been a few seconds ago.

She turned to her source, glancing briefly at Karzai to make sure he was ready. The man she'd been questioning looked suddenly nervous, but she didn't have time to reassure him Axle wouldn't hurt him. "Why do you call him "war"? Is it because he's funding it?"

Karzai translated her question. She couldn't read the man's reply by his expressions this time. He seemed more guarded, so she waited for the answer in English.

"It is his name."

"His name? Is he Russian?"

The man glanced at Axle again. She looked at him then, and he'd inched even closer, practically staring down the man she'd been talking to.

"What are you doing?" she whispered heatedly at him. "Back off." She turned to the villager. "I'm sorry."

"No," Karzai replied. "WAR represents his name. He is

an American soldier." He nodded in Axle's direction. "Dressed like him."

"Shit," Axle breathed.

Jack butted in then. "Caitlin, you're live in ten, nine, eight..."

She quickly thanked the man. "Ask if he can wait here until I'm finished," she said to Karzai before turning to the camera, not able to wait for a confirmation.

"...three...two...one..."

She smiled into the camera as the news anchor read the lead in and tossed it over to her.

"Thank you, Maxwell. I'm in the Achin District in the Nangarhar Province, near the border of Pakistan. On April thirteenth, the United States conducted an air strike utilizing the largest, non-nuclear bomb in its arsenal to take out tunnels used by militant forces, including various factions of the Taliban and ISIS. Just a few miles to the east is where it had been detonated, leveling its target, and branded a success by American and Allied Forces. I have continued to visit area villages and talk with locals to get their take on the covert operation, and the consensus is the same," she said, slowing down her speech with the last few words for a smoother segue into the clip she'd uploaded last night of various interviews, which Jack had edited to fit the timeslot.

She looked to the side, and saw Axle watching her intently. She nodded briefly at him, not wanting to show any emotion while she was in the middle of reporting. She'd be lying to herself if she said she wasn't glad he was the one protecting her. No matter what had happened between the two of them, she knew he was a very skilled warrior and would be safe with him around. She focused on the camera and waited for Jack to count her into the live screen again.

"As you can see behind me," she continued, "the devastation continues even with few people near and military presence practically gone."

"Caitlin, we've received breaking news that there is more to the bombing than first released in the hours after the strike. Can you tell us more about what the townspeople have revealed to you?" Maxwell asked the prepared question.

"Yes. Multiple sources have confirmed that a member of the Shinwari tribe, who has since been identified as Aarif Yasin, was recruited into ISIS and linked to someone selling U.S. military weapons. According to other members of the tribe, Yasin's source was a man going by the name War, who is believed to be a member of the United States military. We have yet to identify War, but he was scheduled to meet Yasin the day of the air strike. I am told Aarif Yasin was killed when the bomb detonated, but the fate of the man he was to meet is unknown.

"In a startling turn of events, we have also learned these tunnels used to move weapons had been a terrorist secret highway, funneling much more than illegally acquired firepower. These underground pathways also provided means to move money that funded rewards for the Taliban. These rewards were offered to them for killing U.S. military personnel. Sources say these contracts were strategically utilized to halt The United States progress...and that they were financially backed by the Russians.

"Were they? If so, how long has this administration been aware of contracts on American lives by a country already accused of manipulation tactics? And if our military knew one of its own had defected, why haven't they released War's identity? Is it because they never wanted the air strike questioned?

"One thing is for certain. There seems to be many parties involved who assumed destroying the extensive tunneling system under these very grounds would bury all the secrets it harbored. This is Caitlin Cooper reporting."

"Fantastic job!" Jack said over her earpiece once she was clear. "We're going to question the president's press secretary at today's briefing. We'll discuss what we find out, and you can report it when we cut to you for the next segment."

"Sounds great." She couldn't stop smiling.

"In the meantime, see what you can find out about War."

"I'm on it," she said, and pulled out her earpiece. She turned toward Karzai and was ecstatic to see the man she'd been questioning was still there. She began walking toward them and said, "We need to ask him about—"

Several loud cracks sounded, startling her. She didn't have time to register what it was because Axle grabbed her and tossed her down behind a half-wall lining the small road. The noise continued, followed by a loud explosion.

Axle did something with his earpiece, but the sounds around them drowned out his words.

Oh God, the cracks. It was gunfire.

Gunfire.

Followed by an explosion, and more shots.

Endless cracks rent the air, going off all around them.

The village was under attack, and they were right in the middle of it! She screamed, grabbing her ears and ducking, acting on self-preservation instinct, but Axle had her covered. He blanketed her so completely, but fear also enveloped her.

"Taking fire!" he shouted, and she rolled her head to the side to look at him. He had his hand to his ear, and she realized he wasn't talking to her. He spoke to his men on the communication device. "Coming from the west... Copy." He rolled off and tugged her arm. "Stay low, follow me." He grabbed her hand and pulled her behind him. Another explosion rocked the center of the village right as they rounded a corner of a building, and both of them ducked lower as they ran.

This was bad. This was very freaking bad! She shook like a leaf, her heart pounding, but she ignored her body's physical reaction to the terror as best she could. "Are we headed to the helicopter?" How close were they to it? She had no sense of direction. Her brain had gone haywire, as chaotic as the scene around them.

"Negative. It's been hit."

She gasped, her head craning instinctively, searching for proof of what happened, as if she needed to confirm they had no way out. Where were Karzai and Lorenzo? The rest of Axle's team? Had they all made it to some kind of shelter, or were they out in the open still? Axle grabbed her hijab and a handful of hair, forcing her back down. She winced and reached for his hand, but dipped back down as he'd instructed.

"Sorry. Stay the fuck down." He pushed the comm, and said, "I see seven tangos to the east. Need to get inside the building. Cover us. Radio in for another helo." So much was happening. She was acutely aware of every sound, probably amplifying them even more. He manacled her wrist and pulled her with him as they ran hunched over to the back of the building beside them. Shots fired in their direction but ricocheted behind them. They found a door, and Axle busted in, taking her with him, his rifle on the ready.

They scanned the barren room with tables and chairs

scattered about, looking for signs of threats. When Axle seemed satisfied they were alone, he turned to her.

"We're in," he said through his communication device, and then said to her, "Are you okay?"

Her mouth fell open, but then she jumped when an explosion outside rocked her. "We're being shot at," she said, her voice rising.

"People tend to do that when you engage in military combat."

"Or maybe they're angry you destroyed their land to eliminate the threat of one of your own people."

Shots continued to fire in the distance. "We don't have time for that right now."

"You wouldn't tell me anyway."

He growled and stormed to a door to check it. When he saw it was only a closet, he turned back to her. "Everybody is on a need-to-know basis. We all have a job to do, and we're not always told every detail or the fucking reasoning behind the decisions being made."

"Did you know? Before your sister translated the video, did you know?"

A sound came from inside the building they were in. Axle put his finger up to his lips in a *be quiet* gesture. He slowly headed in that direction and motioned for her to stay right where she was. He opened the door and went in with warrior stealth.

"Schoolhouse isn't empty."

Schoolhouse? But she could tell from his tone, he wasn't talking to her. She peeked into the room and froze. "Oh no," she breathed, staring down at a dozen or so pair of eyes. She slowly walked all the way in.

He stepped toward the children and motioned with his

hand, instructing them to stay down under their tables. These babies were in this building.

In the middle of a warzone.

Defenseless.

Unfazed.

He glanced around the room, finding a stairwell. "Follow me."

"But the kids," Caitlin said, though she never hesitated to follow him. When they'd first met, she'd bucked his authority at times, but even then she wouldn't have ignored him at a time like this.

That was back when she hadn't had feelings for him.

Trusted him with everything...even something she hadn't planned on giving him.

"Best way to save them is to push back the attack. I need to get higher up and into position. Take out any threat to the kids *and* us."

She looked back at the kids, not wanting to leave them alone.

"C'mon, Caitlin," he said with gentle authority.

They ran up the stairs, not stopping until he found his way onto the roof of the building. It was one of the tallest in the village, but still short enough they could jump from the top. They might break some bones, but they'd survive.

From up here, she could see the devastation. Smoke billowed from four different areas as gunfire continued in a barrage. At this position, the sound reminded her of firecrackers on the Fourth of July, those pesky fireworks that did nothing but pop and crack. It was surreal that sounds of war in a repressed country reminded her of the traditional sounds of celebration on Independence Day. Her brain had a hard time reconciling it with the images of the ruin below.

"Baby, get down," Axle said, pushing on her shoulders

until they were on all fours. The term of endearment caused her already pounding heart to nearly beat out of her chest. She watched him as he crawled to the side, lay on his belly, and propped up his gun, thinking he was too focused on this task of keeping them alive to realize he'd called her anything other than her name.

She followed him, crawling as low to the ground as she could, scraping her elbows and knees through her clothes along the rough and bumpy surface. "What are you going to do from up here? Shouldn't we find the other guys and fight in a group?" She really had no idea how this worked, but there was better luck in numbers, right?

He looked to the side, his eyes cold, fierce. "Too dangerous to run. New transport should be on the way. Air support might have to come if we can't take them out or make 'em retreat. Up here I can keep people from storming the school and using the kids."

"Use the kids? What the hell does that mean?"

His eyes looked troubled for a split second, but whatever the emotion was quickly disappeared before he turned his focus back to the streets. "Our best chance is to stay right here. The team knows where we are. They'll help protect us," he said as he flicked something on his rifle. "Cover your ears," he murmured, the command gentle, which felt all the more foreign. How could he be calm at a time like this?

She quickly slapped her hands over her ears, and Axle pulled the trigger once, the sound blasting through her meekly protected eardrums. Her hands clamped down harder and she ducked her head just as Axle fired another shot. A few seconds later, she looked up at him as he activated his communication device. "Two down. I have four tangos on the move. One running your way, Dozer." He glanced at Caitlin. "Ears."

She covered her ears and flinched when he took another shot, immediately followed by another. About five seconds later, he took two more shots and spoke to his team. "Tangos eliminated... Negative, schoolhouse not breached."

As he continued scanning the area with his scope, he said, "Lorenzo and Karzai entered on the southside of this building and should be covered from fire. AA and Haverty are making their way toward us. When they reach the building, we will head down and rendezvous with them."

"What about the kids?"

"We'll make sure they're safe. Do our best to make sure they live to hate us and try to kill us later."

"Why are you so cynical? Those kids didn't choose this life. Don't you think they should be given a chance to make a change in this world?"

"Don't be so naïve. Children are impressionable. There are now generations of men born and bred to fight in the name of jihad. They are taught from birth Western culture is a threat, and they are to eliminate it." He glanced at her briefly and said, "Those kids don't know any different."

She knew he was right, but she also believed that children could learn from the mistakes of their parents and break the cycle. They were helping make that happen for them. She had to believe they were creating hope for a better life. That in the end, humanity would prevail.

"They will," she said firmly.

"You can lead a horse to water, but you can't make it drink," he said, reciting the old saying as he scanned the area. He fired then, and she covered her ears too late. They rang for several seconds.

When the buzzing stopped, she pulled them back down and said, "They don't even know water is out there. We just have to show them, and they'll figure it out."

His gaze flickered to her for a split second, obviously not wanting to keep his gaze off any incoming threats. "I knew," he said, and she immediately understood he was answering her question from before.

"About killing contracts being funded by the Russians?"

"No. I was aware the tunneling system had been funded by al-Qaeda. That they were used to travel and move anything and everything to assist in their jihad, so money to fund rewards for prices on U.S. military heads could have absolutely funneled through them. I didn't know Russia was involved." He spied her briefly. "Neither do you. That hasn't been confirmed."

"That you know about. You just said we're all on a need-to-know basis."

He shook his head at that. "Cover your ears," he said softly. She did right before he took another shot. Pushing his communication device, he said, "Pathway clear." When he let go, he said, "I can see them. When they reach the building, we gotta bug out. Be ready to move when I say so."

"Okay." He was quiet for several seconds as he viewed the landscape through his scope. "So what *did* you know?"

His jaw clenched. "I was ordered not to help you with your news story."

"And?"

"And, that was before." He said as if that answered the question. She wasn't sure what he meant by that, but her heart screamed it was because *before* he didn't know her.

He'd been ordered before they met. Before he had feelings for her.

"Axle—"

"The defector is Private William Adin Richardson. His initials spell out W.A.R. Weird-ass coincidence or battle-buff parents, I don't know. He was captured and sent to a CIA black site for interrogation."

He'd given her the name. The one she'd sought. The one that would break her story. There was a reason people didn't know much about black sites. They were so classified they were off the books. With that man being held in one, she'd likely never learn his name.

Axle had told her.

"Thank you," she breathed.

"Don't use my name. They're gonna figure out how you found out anyway. I'm the only one on your detail that knows. My SEAL team was briefed on him before we went to the Achin District to scope out the tunnels."

Her mind raced. "I'll find a witness who can corroborate. No one will have to know you're my source."

"You know now. Once we're out of this mess, I'm informing the Major General."

He couldn't do that! He'd get in trouble for sure. "Axle."

"Time to go," he said, getting up quickly and pulling her with him. She tried to argue with him as they raced down the stairs back into the classroom with the children, but he was focused.

The kids hovered around now, no longer under the false safety of their tables. Axle motioned for them to get down as he scanned the area.

Three shots suddenly fired in rapid succession right by her, but they hadn't come from Axle.

Time slowed as those words repeated in her brain...

They. Hadn't. Come. From. Axle.

He roared, and she gasped, turning in the direction of the bullets. But the end of a rifle flew passed her face, barely missing her, tripping her up.

She fell to the ground just as object slammed into Axle's head. Children screamed and ran in various directions.

She scrambled back, trying to figure out what the hell was going on. Had one of the children done this? Had she and Axle fled the dangers of the hardened man only to be taken out by a new generation taught to blindly follow?

She didn't want to believe in lost innocence.

Oh, God. This can't be happening.

Everything happened so fast within the haze of slow motion, but it all had registered. She followed the gun as it was raised from the point of contact with Axle's skull, catching sight of all the blood. His head. His leg. It oozed from several places on his body. The sight of him limp and injured made her wail as tears immediately began to fall.

Axle had been shot.

He'd been knocked out.

God, please let him just be knocked out.

Someone grabbed her hair and tried to yank her up, but when she saw the person standing above her, she gasped. It didn't make sense why she was seeing him right now, here in this room full of children.

Holding a bloody gun.

But he was, and in the instant she saw the shooter, everything changed.

CHAPTER FOURTEEN

"Lorenzo? What the hell?" she screamed, and he let go to aim his gun at her.

"You have no fucking clue what you got yourself into. Sorry, *bella*. Get up."

"What's the matter with you? You shot him!" Screaming at a man with a gun was a stupid idea, but the retort was out before she thought better of it. She scooted away from him, from the children, trying to put some distance between them all and edge closer to Axle. It took everything she had not to look at the man she loved. Because she did. God help her, she was in love with Axle.

If she looked at him, and he was dead, she'd fall apart, like seriously lose it.

"Asad is like a brother to me!" he roared. "No way has he been discharged. No one's heard from him. Those fuckers have him detained somewhere."

He did this because some guy got reassigned? It wouldn't be the first time someone exacted revenge for a job loss, but it was usually the person who'd been canned who went off the deep end.

She needed to figure out how to reason with him, but a part of her told her it wouldn't work. If he'd been willing to shoot someone, Lorenzo was past the point of no return already. He needed professional help. Too bad there wasn't a psychiatrist around. She glanced around the room. *Or another adult.* There was no one else to help her—who was conscious. It would be up to her to find the humanity in him. "That doesn't make any sense, Lorenzo. They don't just detain people for no reason," she said gently.

"He's Aarif Yasin's cousin."

"What?" She frowned at him. How had the man gotten clearance to work with the military if he was related to a possible terrorist? At the very least, this information would've been disclosed.

If they'd known about it.

They must not have. She got the feeling this little detail was learned right about the time he'd been discharged from duty.

She inched closer to Axle until she was sitting against him. When her bottom bumped into this side, he didn't stir.

He made no move at all.

Caitlin bit back a sob. She couldn't lose it. Not right now. She looked at the children again, trying to assess the situation.

They looked terrified.

Earlier, they hadn't been affected by the sounds of war, but this was different.

They weren't involved in whatever Lorenzo was up to. Relief flooded her that she didn't have a roomful of threats, and also because these kids' instincts hadn't been to attack her and Axle as Lorenzo was doing.

"You heard me," he said, and her gaze shot to him. "Why do you think I've been directing you to certain people to interview? Asad had inside info, not that he could come out and share it. It's why I needed him here."

Her mind reeled. "You brought him in to get a *story*?"

"Don't act so high and mighty. When the news breaks about the private involved in the arms deal, you'll be a household name." His words made her sick; her own words earlier about it potentially being the story of her career left her feeling cold. The weird gleam in his eyes only exasperated that negativity. She had journalistic integrity, but in this moment, she felt dirty because of Lorenzo. It didn't matter that the man had lost his marbles, assuming he'd had any to begin with. "You should be thanking me. William Adin Richardson sold out your country, and you get to tell the world."

Yep, he was crazy.

How was she going to get away from him? How was she going to get Axle to safety? She looked around the room again. *How am I going to save these kids?* She wasn't strong enough to move Axle, and he was the only one who knew some of the language. She couldn't communicate anything to the children except some hand gestures. She could run for help. He'd said Acker and Haverty were almost here, but she wasn't leaving Axle. No freaking way. She had to figure something out, and she had to do it quickly.

Lorenzo checked his watch as another explosion rocked the town. A revoltingly sick feeling slid over her. Lorenzo had shot Axle, but no way could he have caused the damage in the village all by himself. "You knew about this attack today." It wasn't a question because she already knew the answer.

A sly smile formed on his face. "Live footage of insurgents is news gold."

"You're sick," she breathed, not sure if he heard her

since the battle raged on in the tiny town, but farther away, thanks to Axle taking out the closer jihadists.

"I'm practical. At least I was until the military up and tossed Asad in some jail. He was my source for years, damn you, years! Now, I need leverage to get him out." He waved the gun as if ordering her to get up.

"You won't get away with this."

He laughed, the sound so sickening she had to swallow the bile that rose in her throat. "I have for years. You think lover boy over there's the first time there's been collateral damage? There's good money in American soldiers."

No, though she didn't have to say it out loud. Her hand brushed along Axle's leg. The cool metal of his sidearm tucked between them made her pulse thunder in her veins. He'd shown her how to use it under life or death circumstances. This totally qualified. If she could just pull it out without Lorenzo seeing...

"Time to go. Move your ass," he said, glancing behind himself.

She had to stall just a little more. "They won't negotiate." She didn't tack on *with terrorists* because she didn't want to offend him with the term.

His face fell a little. "You are a beauty. It'll be a shame when they decapitate you after Asad is freed." He raised his left hand and shut that eye as he regarded her clinically. "I'll make sure the lighting is perfect, and I'll record it from your good side. It'll be so tragically beautiful."

Oh God. No marbles. Not even rolling around at his feet.

He reached for her, and she didn't hesitate. Axle's instructions came back to her in a rush on how to fire the gun. On adrenaline-fueled instinct, she grabbed the gun, pulled it around, and fired several shots. The first and forth ones went wide and up because she'd feared hitting one of the children, but the middle two shots got him, and he fell to the ground. Wow, she'd actually hit him. She'd shot a man. She'd killed him.

She doubted this was what Jack meant when he'd told her, *"Be the story."*

She immediately shoved that thought out of her brain, and she whirled to Axle. She patted along his back, trying not to gag at the blood pooling at his leg. She felt his wrist and almost collapsed over him in relief.

He had a pulse.

She didn't know anything about vital signs or medical care, but she hoped it was strong. *Please, God, let him make it.*

As guns continued to fire outside them, she yanked off her hijab and scarf and quickly worked, tying them around his leg wounds. "Axle, can you hear me?" she asked as she heaved him onto his back. She patted his face and looked along his body for other wounds, feeling a little relief when she didn't find anymore.

He groaned, but didn't move.

"Axle! Axle, wake up. I don't know what the hell I'm doing here." She looked at his ear and the contraption around his neck, wondering how the communication thingy worked. "Please, please, wake up." She cried.

The kids started talking, and her gaze flew toward them. "It's okay," she said as calmly as she could muster. It wasn't okay. None of this was, but she couldn't focus on that right now. She had to come up with a plan.

She looked at Axle again. He still held his rifle. She could try to pull it from him and aim at the door in case anyone rushed the building. If anything, she could keep the kids safe until help arrived. But she wasn't sure if she'd be able to move him enough to get his rifle. *Too bad. You don't have a choice!*

She reached for that big scary gun, but it was strapped to him in a way she couldn't remove it. She wanted to cry. "Wake up," she whispered.

Then his words the night they'd gone to the range came back to her.

"This is my sidearm...I also have a knife here and here," he said, pointing to the one at his belt and one hidden on his ankle... If you need more ammo, here's where I'll have extra magazines."

She grabbed the knife easily visible and dropped it on the floor beside her, but there was blood caked near his foot where he'd pointed that night. She pushed back dark thoughts and got it anyway. Then she patted his chest and made her way down, not sure where the extra magazines would be in his vest thing. Excitement rushed through her when she felt something, and she quickly dug it out. Extra bullets.

"Yes."

And something else. Another weapon he had on him that she hadn't known he'd have. She wasn't sure how much protection it'd provide, but it gave her an odd sense of calm having it in her palm.

The tactical pen.

Feeling her plan click into place, she pocketed the pen and tucked the handgun next to Axle. She picked up both of the knives she'd collected and stood. She still wasn't sure how she was going to tell the children her plan, but she'd do her best. She had no other choice.

"I know you're scared," she said. "I am too, but I'll be damned if anybody *uses* you today." She didn't know how to speak complete sentences in their language, but she said one of the few *Pashto* words she did know, hoping it'd help. "English?"

Most of the children—all boys, she noticed—looked at her without moving. One who was taller than the others nodded.

Relief flooded her. "Do you speak English?" He stared at her, not saying anything. "Do you know what I'm saying?"

His head bobbed as if an agreement.

Good. She could work with that. "Tell your friends they need to get in that closet over there." She extended her arm in a gesture she hoped showed them to gather and follow.

The boy told them in their native tongue, and they all quickly ran to the closet. She held the door as they crowded in.

"Here," she said to the one she'd been instructing. She handed him one of the two knives. She handed the other to the boy standing beside him at the front of the little room. "If a bad man comes, don't let him get you." She started to close the door and then stopped. "I know you don't under-stand everything going on. No one does. I'm sorry." She gave them a sad smile. "One of those guys who came with me or I will come get you when it's safe. Stay here, okay?" She didn't wait for answer. She wasn't even sure if the boy who knew some English understood everything she'd just said.

Once the children were in a slightly safer place, she rushed back to Axle's side, but jolted to a stop at what she saw.

"No," she breathed. "I thought I killed you."

———

AXLE'S LEG SCREAMED. Pain burned, but he had difficulty figuring out why. The ringing in his ears wasn't helping at all.

Noise got louder, and he stirred, trying to make sense of what happened. His leg wasn't actually screaming, but somebody was. Why couldn't he make his body work?

Someone touched him, and the scent of Caitlin washed over him. He loved the way she smelled. The way she tasted. The way she glared at him when he made her mad. God, he loved everything about her.

He loved her.

She said something to him, and he tried to respond, but he felt so heavy. Like he was dreaming but trying to move in real life. Maybe he was asleep with her lying beside him. He groaned at the thought of holding her to him and being lazy together all day. He couldn't wait to feel her underneath him again...whenever he woke up.

"You have bad aim," someone who sounded like Lorenzo said. Why was he dreaming about the cameraman? The man was probably going to flirt with Caitlin in his dream. This was a nightmare for sure. "Where's your gun?"

He didn't know where it was.

"I don't have it," Caitlin said.

Axle frowned at that.

"Looks like your bodyguard's waking up. Think I'll have some fun before I shoot him again."

Fire laced through burning leg and the roar he'd tried to get out earlier finally came free as he broke through the fog of unconsciousness. He jolted up, hands slapping the ground beside him to find purchase, his left one landing on something cold and hard. His gaze, though, was on the foot crushing his wound.

The war.

The gunfire.

Caitlin.

It all came crashing back. Years of training, of shooting practice and torture drills, of real-life scenarios putting his skills to the test, kicked in.

Lorenzo was a threat.

The cold steel under his hand was his handgun. He wasn't a natural lefty, but he could shoot hanging upside down in a sandstorm.

He also knew he had one mother of a concussion.

That was fine. He could account for that. Channeling all of his strength and speed, he shut one eye to alleviate his double vision and growled out loud, hoping Lorenzo would take it as that of pain when he'd actually wanted to cover the sound of shifting the gun to get a good grip on it.

"Stop," Caitlin screamed, and her steps sounded closer than before. "Let's just go. You wanted to use me as leverage. You don't have to hurt him."

"I'm not leaving a payday behind."

Lorenzo wasn't taking her anywhere. He'd have to kill Axle first.

With practiced stealth, he raised the gun, but Caitlin lunged for Lorenzo. She hit him with something small in his arm, and he roared, turning his gun on her. Axle didn't hesitate. He fired one, hitting Lorenzo in the head. He crumpled to the floor, and Axle fell back to the ground, trying to fight off the darkness. "Caitlin," he breathed.

"Axle," she yelled. Her hands traced his body. "I-I stuck him with your pen. You've been shot. The kids are—"

A door slammed, stopping her words or drowning them out, he wasn't sure.

Caitlin gasped, and he tried to open his eyes. He would not let anyone else get to her. He didn't know how, but he'd put himself between her and whoever the new threat was. He raised the gun in the direction.

"Easy," Alec said.

"AA?" she asked, and Axle didn't have to have his eyes open to know his team had made it to them. He dropped his weapon.

"That's Double Alpha to you," he said as he rushed toward them. "You did good, Sweet Pea." He inspected what felt like a makeshift bandage. "Axle's down. Need med evac."

Axle squeezed his eyes. "Don't flirt with her," he breathed.

"Axle!" She stroked his face.

"Wouldn't dream of it, Sir. Haverty's on his way up to help me carry you. Don't shoot him."

"Fuck you," he breathed, opening his eyes. He still saw double of everything. Except Caitlin. She seemed to be vibrating.

"Baby," he breathed.

Acker looked at her. "Shit. You're okay. Just a little shock. Stay with me, Sweet Pea."

"I'm just shaking a little."

"C'mon. Axle needs us. And if you pass out, I'll have to leave him here bleeding out to deal with you first. Doesn't matter he needs medical attention. If I extracted him first, he'd have my ass."

She raised her hand to her head to try to salute him in that awful why she'd been doing since she got here.

He chuckled. "You're bad at that."

"So I've heard," she said, but the words were broken, which jolted Axle. He rose up in time to catch her as she passed out, taking them back to the ground, but him cushioning her fall.

"I'm going to need more help up here," Alec said to someone.

Axle held her to him, hating he couldn't carry her out on his own. He'd shield her, though. No way was he going to let any more danger come after her. He had to protect her no matter the cost.

And he would. She meant too much to him not to. Oh, he'd tried to deny how he felt. Even pushed her away to keep them from getting even more attached. He'd tried to keep from falling deeper into his feelings. He'd fought himself every step of the way.

It was a battle not meant to be won.

CHAPTER FIFTEEN

"If you don't let me do this on my own, I'm going to kick your butt," Axle said to Shelby when she reached for him.

"Let him do it himself, love," Mason said. After getting out of surgery, he'd had a cast on his leg and had been healing at his sister's house.

Her new house.

She'd been staying in an FBI safehouse before he'd gotten shot, but sometime between his surgery in a German hospital and his arriving stateside for final debriefing, she'd decided she needed a bigger place so Axle could have plenty of room to recover with her. He'd need time and space to go through physical therapy to work on his atrophied muscles, and there weren't too many opportunities for her to baby her big brother. It seemed she loved every second of it.

"Yeah, let me do it myself," he said, agreeing with Mason as he took another step. He'd gotten to know the guy his sister had fallen in love with over these last couple of months. Although he had a sense of authority about him that Axle had the natural instinct to challenge—the man was his sister's boyfriend, after all—he did like him. When his sister had told him more details of how they'd found love on assignment, Axle had wanted to choke the man. If he hadn't been on some killer pain medication, he would've tried, but as time went on, he saw how much the man loved Shelby.

So much so that he'd bought her this house. No way could Shelby afford a place like this on her own. She wasn't drawing a paycheck from the feds, and what she made at the garage couldn't be anywhere near enough to qualify for the type of loan she would've needed. When they'd first pulled up to the electric gate, he'd almost jokingly asked her whose dick she'd had to suck to get a place like this, but since they'd had words about her last assignment already, he'd thought better of it. Besides, he didn't want her taking the comment seriously. He'd just eyed her as they waited for the gate to open after she'd typed in the code, and she'd shrugged it off with a sly smile.

He didn't have to ask to know the truth.

And what right did he have to question her or anyone else on fraternizing or crossing professional lines of obligation.

He'd been ordered to protect a woman, and he'd slept with her.

He'd been ordered not to tell her shit, and he'd given her classified information.

It didn't matter if he'd protected her in the end. That she'd gotten out of a warzone unharmed and had completed her assignment. He'd gone against his superiors.

There had only been one thing he could do about it.

He'd confessed it all to Major General Burge.

Oh, the ass chewing he'd gotten was of Biblical proportions. He had no doubt if he hadn't been lying injured in a hospital bed, he would've faced court-martial. A shitty end to a career spanning years. From early military, to SEALs, to joint taskforce operations, it could have easily all come down to an unceremonious *fuck-you* exit.

Getting injured had been his saving grace. He couldn't very well be allowed back to active duty when he could barely walk. By the time he healed enough to return, his service would be over anyway. When he'd held Caitlin on that schoolhouse floor, the world in chaos around them, he'd known then he wouldn't be reupping even if he could. A few months without her while he completed his remaining service obligation was much easier to cope with than years under a new contract could possibly be.

He'd already decided to pursue a new chapter in his life before he got the news of how much damage there'd been to his leg, which would've made the decision for him. Since he was leaving the military, there hadn't been a reason for Burge to make a stink about Axle giving Caitlin that name.

He took another step, and the physical therapist corrected his posture. "Told you I could do it," he muttered.

"You're doing so good. I'm so proud of you," she squealed.

"Jesus, I'm not a baby."

The intercom buzzed, drawing all of their attention. "Someone's at the gate," Mason said. He gave his sister a kiss and left the room. She stared after him, smiling goofy.

"You're supposed to pay attention to me," he said.

"And you said you're not a baby. Sure are whining like one."

The physical therapist smiled. She was pretty. If he'd been in a different place in his life, he'd have asked her out. Those days were over, and it had nothing to do with his probable life-long disability.

"Am not," he said, continuing with their juvenile banter.

"Are so."

He took another step and another. His leg ached, but he was determined to get it working as best he could.

"Good work, Mr. Landry. We'll do some ice therapy to get the swelling down and be done for the day." She helped him lay on the foam table Shelby had set up in this large space. She'd said she needed a workout room anyway, which just so happened to include all the machinery he'd need for his therapy sessions and exercising his leg. When he expressed doubt she'd be working out so much she would need a cold therapy machine, she'd made a dirty joke about playing with it once he was done. Mason had cracked a smile, and Axle really hadn't wanted to ask what she'd meant by that.

"Look who I found," Mason said as he walked back into the room.

Oz and Zeke walked in with another guy. Shelby waved at him, but he was too stunned to ask who that person was.

"Holy shit," Axle breathed. He hadn't seen these guys in years. Not since their Orion mission.

"Damn, brother, always lying on your ass," Zeke said.

Axle laughed and clapped him on the back when he leaned over to hug him.

Oz shook his hand. "Good to see you. Sorry it's not under better circumstances."

"Nah, man. We've all been busy. While I've been getting shot, Zeke's been pushing papers, and you've been playing house."

"Ah, fuck you, man," Zeke said. "I run my own FBI team."

"Like I said, paper pusher." Oz cracked a smile, and Axle asked him, "How's the wife?"

His smile widened. "Good. Really good. She's home with the kids."

"What? You got kids, man? That's awesome." Oz had fallen in love with Bryn, a woman who'd been on the run from the mafia, and he'd been in charge of watching.

Oh the irony.

Axle had given Oz so much shit about Bryn back then and here he was, head over heels for the woman he'd been ordered to protect.

"Yeah. It is."

He looked at the other guy in the room with them. He resembled Oz, and Axle realized who it probably was. "You must be Gauge," he said.

"I am." He walked over and shook his hand. "I, uh, wanted to meet you and tell you I'm sorry for getting you into all of this," he said, shoving his hands into his pockets.

Axle nodded at him. "Not your fault, man." He looked at Shelby. "Not yours either."

Her lips quivered, and Mason seemed to materialize at her side, rubbing her back, immediately comforting her. She'd taken him getting shot pretty hard. Not only was he her brother, and she the one to initially suggest he be the one assigned to Caitlin, but she herself had been shot before and knew the pain involved. Thankfully, her wound hadn't been as bad as his. Not physically anyway. Shelby had been dealing with much more than pain of the flesh, but he could tell she was doing much better than just a few months ago.

"You never said your sister was so hot," Zeke said, trying to lighten the mood, but when Mason's gaze shot to him, it was apparent the attempt had failed miserably. "Sorry, guy."

"She's mean as hell anyway," Gauge said, smiling and

not caring Mason trained his protective gaze on him now. He looked at Axle. "I work with her. I'm allowed to say that."

"Because you're an agent?" he asked.

"No. Well, yeah," he said, frowning slightly. "My career is a little more complex than that."

"I'm not going anywhere," Axle said, indicating the machine he was hooked up to.

"Miss, can you excuse us a minute?" Oz asked the physical therapist.

Mason walked toward her and escorted her out. Shelby stepped over to Axle and sat on the edge of the bed.

"You know I was investigating the Bang Shift, right?"

"Yeah," he said slowly.

"The feds had assigned Gauge to work deep undercover as a member of their group. Eventually, the government sussed out their bad guy, but Gauge stayed on when Xan decided to stay in Mayflower."

"Xan?"

"Alexandra Collins," Oz said, penning him with a knowing stare.

"What?" Axle asked slowly. "Marco's ex isn't in WINSEC anymore?" That had been the catalyst for Orion's first—and only—mission.

"It's Xan Jackson, now, and her husband and his friends won't let anybody near her," Gauge said with an odd finality. "The Bang Shift can protect her better than some overworked case manager."

"Long story short," Shelby said. "The Bang Shift isn't only a garage. They're hired guns. If the feds pay them to handle other matters, they shouldn't have a problem with them taking care of this one for free."

He knew there had to be a valid reason for Shelby to

investigate them before, and this made sense. Then he glared at her as something else clicked into place. "So you're not just rotating tires for them?"

"I mean...I do that, too."

"That's actually the other reason we're here," Gauge said.

"I'm listening," he said, trying not to be irritated with anybody else other than his sister.

"They need your help," Oz said.

Axle chuckled. "I hope it doesn't require running because you'd be shit outta luck."

"You're supposed to let me do the talking," Gauge said.

"You're beating around the bush," Oz retorted.

"Yep, y'all are definitely brothers," Axle muttered.

"What's that supposed to mean?" Shelby asked, rearing back.

"That siblings can be a pain in the ass."

"Jesus, we're gonna be here all day," Zeke said.

Mason walked back into the room. "Why does everybody look like they're gonna start shooting?" he joked, but there was a hard glint in his eyes.

"Get her outta here, please," Axle said to him as he pointed at Shelby.

"You don't have to be such a jerk."

"See, mean, I told ya," Gauge said to Mason.

"Nobody's going anywhere," Mason said calmingly as he walked farther into the room. He reached Shelby and kissed the top of her head.

"Anyway," she said slowly. "We think you should come work with us."

"I was supposed—ugh," Gauge said, stopping on a groan.

"Fuck, man, your balls not drop yet?" Oz asked, shaking

his head. He turned to Axle. "This is perfect. You have garage experience, so you can work at the shop, and you have a long military background working reconnaissance missions, so you can take on contracts. You're not just comfortable with a gun. You're the fucking best."

He blinked, not sure what to say.

"Don't let the idea of working with me stop you," Shelby said with a wink. She was a brat, but he did love her.

"You'll be doing me a huge favor," Gauge said.

Axle shook his head. "I'm all outta favors. Still working on my last one." He nodded at his leg.

"You want to blame someone, take it out on me," Oz said. "I was the one Gauge called when Shelby first mentioned you doing it. I agreed with him, and I called in the favor."

"Look, I'm not mad about being assigned to Caitlin," he said, trying not to show any emotion at voicing her name aloud, "But I'm not clear how you calling in a favor to protect a woman you don't even know somehow meant involving me. We haven't seen each other in years."

"Because it mattered enough to your sister to protect her friend. Because you're the best goddamn shooter I know—"

"Hey," Zeke said, acting offended.

"And our father," Oz continued, pointing at himself and Gauge, "took a bullet meant for Burge."

The life debt. That made complete sense.

"I never thought you'd get hurt," Shelby said.

Axle sighed. "I'll heal. Stop feeling guilty." He turned to Gauge. "I get it, and thanks for the offer, but I don't need charity."

"It's not charity. We're swamped. We have cars booked

out for months. Brody's wife is about to have a baby, so we can't even entertain other jobs right now."

"Sorry, man. I can't do shit as it is anyway. I'll figure out what I'm going to do with my life when I get better." And it would probably entail finding a job in Atlanta...for reasons he didn't want to dive too far into.

"By Brody's wife, he means the woman formerly known as Alexandria Collins," Oz said. "Remember her former nanny? The woman who helped raise her son, Scott? The woman I later married? Well, she's tired of letting the mafia control her life. She wants to move to this little town, see this baby grow up, be a part of Scott's life."

"Oh shit," Axle said.

"Yeah, which means, these two women who should be on opposite ends of the world to keep the mafia from ever finding them are going to be living in the same tiny town."

Gauge winced. "Sorry. I never should've said anything. I thought she'd be happy to hear how well Xan was doing. I didn't think..."

"I'll deal with you later," Oz grumbled.

"This is why I need the favor," Gauge said. "We need help, sure. I mean, it's not like we can run an ad online that says, *Help wanted. Must be good with torque guns and shotguns.* But with my sister-in-law wanting to move here, maybe my brother won't kill me if there's an *assassin* on the team."

"It's sniper, not assassin," Axle corrected.

"Assassin sounds cooler."

"He has a point," Zeke said. "And those *other jobs*, he mentioned? He meant the feds. I have a case I need them to work on, but they're reluctant," he said, drawing out the last word.

"Well, the FBI should handle their own shit," Axle said.

"Quit spending government dollars on contractors and get people on the payroll to do their jobs."

"You're right," Zeke said, but his tone belied any real agreement. "Absolutely right. I'll just run on down to Quantico and get someone green."

"Why don't you call Katie Dean?" Axle asked sarcastically, not liking his attitude and purposely pushing an off-limits button by bringing up the woman Zeke had a major thing for.

"Good idea," he said without missing a beat. "She probably won't be such a little bitch when she's asked to protect Caitlin Cooper."

His former teammate was out for blood. Zeke's thing for Katie might be something long buried, but Axle's feelings for Caitlin were fresh.

They'd never fade.

"I did not complain when I was given that assignment!" Yes, he'd been mad getting pulled from his SEAL team, but he'd taken the role without any lip.

"Bub," Shelby said softly. "He's not talking about before."

"What. The. Fuck?" he asked, low and deadly.

"She'll be here in three weeks."

CHAPTER SIXTEEN

Today.

Caitlin Cooper sat nervously as she gazed over the crowd. There were more people here than she'd anticipated, though a Bronze Star Ceremony was sure to be the talk of the town and draw even those normally uninterested in current affairs out of the woodwork. When Caitlin's gaze landed on a group of tough-looking men entering the room, she quickly dropped it to her notebook as heat tinged the tips of her ears. Only one man caused that reaction. Unable to resist his pull, she looked at him again.

Axle stared right at her.

Caitlin swallowed, locked in his hot gaze, instantly taken back to *other* times he'd looked at her just as intensely but for a completely different reason. She couldn't look away now even if she wanted to, and she didn't. She'd missed him so much since the last day she saw him...the day everything went to shit, and they'd been ripped apart by circumstance.

He took a step, then another, slowly making his way to the stage without breaking eye contact just yet. She wanted to run to him and help him walk, but she knew beyond any doubt he'd hate her even more if she offered him any assistance. He was a strong man.

He was a proud man.

And now, he was a disabled man. A former SEAL injured in the prime of his life. The career he carefully nurtured for so many years completely obliterated.

All because of her.

More than anything else, that killed her. She loved him. Even not seeing him these last few months, her feelings hadn't changed. If anything, they'd grown stronger.

When he reached the stage, she stood and watched as he held onto the handrail, making his way toward the center. She wanted to run to him, but she couldn't. Not with the whole town crammed into this room, watching.

The governor made his way to the podium, and Caitlin took her seat. It was time for the ceremony to start anyway. The governor went through the pomp and circumstance of his speech, and all she could think about was that last day with Axle. At the beginning of the day, she'd been high on the story break she'd gotten while also hurting for Axle, knowing their time together was coming to an end. By the end of the day, she'd been frantically trying to see him in the medical ward. Alec—AA—had told her he'd call her as soon as Axle's condition stabilized. She'd been shoved onto the first plane out of the country, and by the time she landed in Dubai, she'd had a voicemail telling her Axle had made it out of his first surgery. AA had called her a couple more times over the next week with updates. Then he'd gone onto another assignment, and Axle was sent home to recover from his injuries. She had no idea if he'd been medically discharged or was on leave. Thanks to HIPAA and the impenetrable wall of the military, she'd been unable to find out specifically. She had theories based on research. It wasn't as if she could reach out to Axle and ask. Even if she knew his number, he'd made it clear before he'd gotten hurt that he didn't want anything to do with her.

And then he'd gotten injured.

All because of her.

If she hadn't gone, he wouldn't have been put on a special assignment to protect her. Nor would he have been forced to work in the same proximity as the madman colleague of hers. Axle was a hardened special ops. She could only imagine the battles he fought for the greater good, and he'd taken several bullets because someone thought dramatizing the war made for good news clips. She was surprised Axle even looked at her today.

She could only image how much hatred he felt toward her. She didn't want to think about it, actually. It was why she'd only asked Heather a couple of times to find out his status. Once she knew he was doing better, she had to do whatever she could to give him the space he'd asked for.

He'd sacrificed for.

And here he was, still sacrificing himself for the sake of her.

"...So it's my esteemed pleasure to introduce Axle Landry." The governor turned to Axle and clapped as the audience gave him a standing ovation. Caitlin swallowed, her heart pounding as she watched him make his way to the podium.

He shook the governor's hand, thanked the audience, and graciously asked them to take their seats. After several moments, they finally complied. "It's great to be here today. Arkansas is a pretty damn good state." Another round of applause with some whooping from the audience. He laughed, seemingly lighthearted, and it was music to Caitlin's ears. He hadn't shown her an easygoing side of himself, but then again, they'd been in the middle of a warzone.

Since she could stare at him unabashedly, she drank him in. He looked good in his dress uniform. Damn good. He still looked tough with an air of authority. Even hobbling slightly, he still pulled it off. But the uniform, that was such a contradiction to all images she had of him. He'd always worn military fatigues. Except when he had nothing on at all.

She shoved that thought away as fast as it formed.

Axle continued with his speech, discussing his time in the military, his service to this country, and the horrors of war. She listened, his words beautiful even when the topic held such devastating consequences. Then he looked at her.

The air in her lungs locked.

"This isn't about me, though. When I got asked to speak today, I was truly humbled. Caitlin Cooper is one of the bravest people I know, and that includes some of the toughest men and women I've served alongside. Without her, I wouldn't be standing here before you, and a roomful of children might not have lived to one day make a difference in this world. She taught me that," he said slowly, and looked back toward the audience. Tears threatened at the sincerity of his words. "I'm so incredibly honored to be a part of her big day and will forever treasure witnessing her receiving the Bronze Star Medal."

People clapped and Axle joined in, watching her. Caitlin blushed, but she couldn't look away from him, as she was transfixed in his gaze. She didn't agree with his words, but she appreciated him making this easier. He could have stood up and told it like it was without sugarcoating the reality.

He was too good of a man to do that.

Axle had been awarded the highest award for his actions in the battle. He'd been the one to take out the threats to those children. If it hadn't been for him doing that, there would've been no need for her to shuttle them into a closet. Saving those children—and her—had earned him the Medal of Honor. She'd been so proud of him when she'd heard the news. She couldn't count the number of times she watched online clips of the president awarding it to him. He very much deserved the recognition. Caitlin, however, felt like a hack. She hadn't been the one putting her life on the line for others. She'd been a nervous wreck, shot her colleague and then stabbed him, and *then* passed out. She hadn't even been able to leave the building that day on her own two feet.

Neither had he, the voice in her head taunted. That little voice of reason had been busy ever since she learned the news of this award a few weeks ago. She hadn't felt worthy, but then she figured most people who received recognition didn't.

When Axle finished, she mouthed, "Thank you." His words meant more to her than the medal itself.

He inclined his head before an officer stood and shook his hand, dismissing him from his speech. Caitlin rose and went to the center as instructed. The officer completed the ceremony, and with practiced precision, she saluted him. Unable to stop herself, she glanced at Axle. He had a look of pride, and she knew she'd nailed it. Lord knew she'd practiced a bazillion times. Joy and nerves mingled as she started in on the small speech she'd prepared. Her voice shook, but she did her best to get through it without breaking down.

"...No one is ever prepared to see the devastation of war. There are men and women who face terror head-on every day. We honor those who served on Veteran's Day. We remember those who lost their lives on Memorial Day. But the rest of time, we civilians carry on with our lives not thinking much about the freedom they protect. I wasn't selfless that day. Alec Acker, Pierce Haverty, Brooks Chamberlain, Ryder Lawrence, Logan Hardwick, Kayden Wright, and Axle Landry were," she said, making sure to look at Axle when she said his name from the list of men assigned to her protection. She was grateful, of course, but in the end, all she'd done was protect the man she loved when he couldn't do it himself.

There was an awkward silence. Had she veered off script and said that last part out loud? Her gaze shot to Axle. His eyes flared. She cleared her throat and looked at her notes, the last spoken words drifting through her head, *"All I did was protect the man I love."* She had said it. Oh, God. "Um, the man who protected me," she said immediately, and continued with the carefully crafted words as if she'd never made that confession. To a room full of people. She glanced at her parents as she spoke. Her dad was so proud he probably hadn't even heard what she said. Her mom, on the other hand, had a knowing look in her eyes. Caitlin's gaze darted away from the compassionate scrutiny.

When she finished, the crowd cheered, and she couldn't help but smile in gratitude as she stepped off the stage. She shook hands with the people closest to her before branching out and greeting many of the local townspeople. Most of the other guys on her detail had been overseas, but AA and Brooks where there and hugged her.

Her parents gushed all over her, but quickly moved away so she could continue thanking people. When the lieutenant governor reached for her hand, she started. Then she hated he'd caught her unawares. She'd seen him earlier, knew he was here, but she had hoped to avoid him. When he pulled her closer, she wanted to balk, remembering how he'd trapped her all those years ago when he'd been an aide. She hid her reaction and locked her knees to keep professional pretenses since people were standing all around.

"You're looking lovely as always, Cait. How about dinner later, so I can show you proper appreciation?"

"Let. Go."

The command was decisive, but it hadn't come from her.

She could feel Axle's body heat from behind. God, that voice of his melted her in all the right places. She wanted to sink into his warmth, but she couldn't ever do that again. He was here because he'd been asked to speak. He'd smiled and been courteous, but there wasn't anything between them, and she'd do right to remember that.

The jerk holding her hand dropped it and glanced around, smiling nervously and obviously hoping he hadn't caused a scene with his constituents.

"You ever come near her again, I'll kill you myself," he whispered. Then he reached out, grabbed the man's hand and shook it. "Thank you, Sir," he said with fake enthusiasm, probably keeping up pretenses of a more civilized conversation. The slime ball walked away.

"Thank you," she said without turning toward Axle.

"He's lucky I didn't call in a sniper the day you told me he'd made you uncomfortable on the job." She'd forgotten about that. They'd been talking about his sister and something to do with sexual harassment.

He had an amazing memory.

Everything about him was.

His hand landed on her shoulder. Her eyes drifted close, but she quickly opened them, not wanting to get lost in this man, as he turned her to face him.

He opened his mouth to speak, but the heat in his gaze had her scrambling to stop what he was about to say. More nerves? Definitely.

"How's your leg?"

He smiled slowly. "Hurts like a sonofabitch."

She winced. "I'm sorry."

His eyes popped, and then his brow furrowed. "You say that like it's your fault."

"Well, it is. I mean, you were protecting me when it—"

"Jesus, between you and Shelby…" He drifted off, shaking his head. "Why do I have the feeling if I tell you it comes with the job, it won't ease whatever screwed up blame you've got going on?"

"Because it won't."

"Hell, Caitlin, that wasn't the first time I've been shot. Or the second. And those are just wounds I've endured from the business end of a gun, not counting all the other kinds of injuries I gotten over the years."

She hadn't thought about it like that, not that she relished the idea of him being seriously injured multiple times in his career.

"I had a dangerous job. One I loved for a long time. Believe me, I'm proud of my service. My scars are badges. Now that I've been discharged, they're reminders of all the good I did for people."

"Oh God," she breathed. He'd been discharged because of the injury. She'd worried about that, and now he confirmed that horrible fear.

He leaned onto his cane and cupped her cheek with his free hand. "I'm alive because of you."

"You're hurt because of—"

His mouth landed on hers, and she gasped at the sudden contact. All that did was give him an opening to deepen the kiss, and all worries about causing him harm fled...at least in this moment. He tasted of mouthwash and tea and so much potential that she shook as she finally allowed herself to lean into him and hold on for dear life.

Because life was dear. They'd both been close to losing that precious thing.

When he broke away, he said hoarsely, "Did you mean what you said? No, don't answer that." He laughed gently. "I love you, too. If either of us owes the other an apology, I'm the one who should be doing the groveling. I pushed you away because my feelings were a distraction to your safety. I couldn't allow anything to happen to you. I'd rather hurt a thousand times than you feel pain in the slightest. If anything had happened to you because I wasn't on my A game, I wouldn't be able to live with myself. That's how precious you'd become to me."

"Axle," she said on a light breath.

"It happened so fast. You slipped into the desert and crashed right into my heart. I've never felt this way about anyone. Ever."

"Me too."

He kissed her again. God, she'd missed him so much.

A throat cleared beside them.

With a groan, Axle pulled away. "What?" he barked at the man who'd interrupted them.

Hunter Anderson. She leaned her head on Axle's chest and wanted to laugh that her childhood crush had no effects on her libido. Oh, time was a wonderful thing.

"I want to congratulate my old friend here," Hunter said, pulling her out of Axle's arms into a bear hug. "Heather is—"

"Right here," Heather squealed, and yanked her out of Hunter's arms and into hers. "I'm so proud of you." She pulled back. "Don't ever do something like that again!" She crushed Caitlin to her again. "But I'm so proud of you."

"Thank you," Caitlin said with a laugh. "But it was my job." The words so similar to Axle's clicked into place. He'd been doing his job when he'd gotten hurt, and Caitlin just told Heather the danger of her job was worth the risk.

"And you did an amazing one. That piece on the military cover-up of the arms deal went viral. And that Russian bit? Holy cow! Story of your career, girl."

A journalist's dream. Afterward, she'd become the one being interviewed on the talk show circuit because everyone wanted to hear about *her* experience. It had been surreal. Breaking that story had changed everything.

Heather leaned back. "Wait a minute. What do you mean *was* your job?"

Caitlin winced. She hadn't told anyone back home about her new job with a local station. When she'd been offered the nightly news anchor position, she'd thought *WWCAD?* And had promptly decided her icon would ride the high of publicity and take the wonderful desk job. Caitlin still battled with nightmares, and she wasn't sure when she'd feel comfortable reporting live from a warzone again...if ever. Truth was, she'd missed Arkansas. She missed home.

"You're looking at the new anchor for Channel 4 News at six and ten."

"Oh my gosh!" Heather said in a rush.

"Yeah."

"Oh my gosh!" she said again even louder.

"Yeah," Caitlin repeated on a chuckle. "I'm moving back."

Heather squealed in earnest. Caitlin felt her joy down to her toes. She wanted to steal a glance at Axle to gauge his reaction, but she was too chicken. They hadn't decided anything. Just because they loved each other—

Caitlin gasped as she was ripped from Heather's arms and crushed into the welcoming chest she'd missed so much. "Thank fuck," he breathed.

"Well, this is great news," some other guy said. She didn't have to know who it was to know he'd been happy to hear this news. She was about to ask him why he cared about her job, but he turned to Axle. "You have no reason to turn me down now."

Huh?

"Yeah," Axle said. "We'll talk, Gauge."

You'll talk about what?

"Awesome, man." Caitlin watched as Hunter clapped Axle's shoulder. "We'll give you some privacy." He clutched Heather. She pouted as she was dragged away by her brother. She smiled at her friend and looked up into Axle's eyes.

"What are you going to talk about?"

"Gauge offered me a job with The Bang Shift."

She gaped at him. "You know what they do, right? I mean, besides the car stuff?" She'd been shocked to learn Hunter was a mercenary, and it had angered her to think Axle had been one, too. Funny how time...and feelings...and near death experiences...changed things.

"Yeah. He told me."

She laughed then, remembering how mad she'd gotten.

"I was so pissed when I thought you'd been hired to protect me and not assigned."

He chuckled. "Technically, I was paid." He shrugged. "Anyway, I told him no at first. Then he told me you were coming here when the ceremony finalized. The feds needed extra protection since you decided to rock the world with your breaking news."

"Can't help it I'm good." She winked.

"Yes, yes, you are." He kissed her swiftly.

"So you're here to protect me?"

"Of course. And then when the organizers found out I'd be here, they asked if I wanted to speak. Told them I'd be honored."

She smiled up at him. "So this was like your job interview."

"Yeah. He wasn't happy I'd told him I had to think about it because, well, I was entertaining a job offer in Atlanta," he said pointedly.

"You were going to move by me." It wasn't a question, and the knowledge left her all warm inside. He loved her. He truly did.

"Hard to be with you if I didn't. Out of the two of us, I'm the most flexible job-wise right now, though you just made my decision pretty damn easy."

Happiness for her, for this man, bloomed within. She could see herself spending the rest of her life with him, and the way he looked at her, it was a safe bet he felt the same way.

"And you're okay working with Hunter?"

Axle's eyes narrowed, but a smile slowly formed. "Gotta keep an eye on your old boyfriend."

"What? I told you we didn't have a thing," she said quickly.

"Mmm," he said, obviously not quite convinced. "That's good because I'm a territorial S.O.B."

"Lots of little girls have crushes. Then we grow up."

His eyes twinkled. "I'm sure you were completely adorable."

"Yeah, not the word I'd pick to describe it." She shrugged. "So you're cool with working for him? Doing the job, I mean."

Axle stroked her arm, and goosebumps erupted along the path. "I have a special skillset. There's a lot going on that we need to talk about. Dangers that can come knocking. But today is your day. We have plenty of time to get into all of that."

"Okay," she said slowly, not really sure what to think about that. A more important question was pressing, and she leaned in a little, wanting to tease him. "But tell me something. What makes you think you'll even like me once you get to know me?"

He cocked an eyebrow. "Oh, I know you very intimately."

She swung her palm against his chest. "I'm serious. I might snore."

"Oh, you do. Just because I never slept in that room with you doesn't mean I didn't come in while you were sleeping. That nose is like a freight train." He winced playfully as he tweaked it.

She rolled her eyes. "You just like it when I play with your gun," she said, remembering the time they'd slipped into innuendo, but then her smile dropped. She'd had to use his gun for real. The scene had played out in bloody detail over and over in the darkest part of her nights.

"Hey," he said softly as he tucked a strand of hair behind her ear. The kindness in his eyes almost undid her.

With the same gentle tone, he said, "You can't shoot for shit."

She burst out laughing, and he chuckled, breaking his straight face.

"Oh, I got something for you." He stepped back, digging in his pocket.

"I bet you do," she said teasingly but with loads of suggestion.

He growled playfully. She really liked this easygoing side of his. She looked forward to learning all his sides.

"Here." He handed her a long jewelry box, like ones that housed a bracelet or anklet. "To commemorate your special day."

She reached for it, her heart racing once again as she opened it. Oh, she loved jewelry just like the next woman, but this was too much—

Caitlin's laugh was so sudden it shocked her.

"Your very own tactical pen. Complete with a handcuff key. Mine doesn't even that have."

"I love it," she said, smiling like a fool and not even caring. "It's perfect."

He reached for her, and Caitlin knew she'd never tire of having his arms around her.

"It's dangerous, which is the point. But if you ever attack me with one of these again, I'll haul you over my knees and spank your ass."

It was her turn to make a sexy sound at the back of her throat.

He groaned. "Jesus, I was going to ask you out to eat, so we can get this dating thing going. But all I want to do is drag you back to my hotel and have you six ways to Sunday."

She smiled coyly. "Why don't you try asking me anyway?"

Axle smiled, but there was a slight crinkle between his brows as he seemed to wonder what she was getting at. "Okay, baby. What would you like to eat? We can have anything you want."

Caitlin leaned close and whispered in his ear, "Breakfast."

He gasped and crushed his mouth to hers as she giggled, her humor dying as he kissed her passionately, adoringly.

From the foothills of the Ozarks to the mountains of Afghanistan, she'd always chased the story, never expecting to find love. Yeah, she'd scooped the story of her career, but with Axle, she'd landed the story of her life.

"To THE NEW anchor for Channel 4 News at six!" Heather said, raising her glass to toast Caitlin on her new job. The last couple of weeks had been a whirlwind getting her moved from Atlanta to Mayflower, so this was the first time they'd all had a chance to get together. The girls anyway.

"And ten," Shelby added. "The new anchor for Channel 4 News at six and ten."

Maya had come along since she was one Caitlin's good friends. They were still getting to know Shelby, but she seemed pretty cool. Since she worked with Heather's brother, and Caitlin dated Shelby's brother, it seemed fitting to have her here with them.

Heather had asked Xan if she wanted to come along, too, but she was about to pop that baby out. Roxie refused to join them for the same reason. Heather just knew Brody would have a time on his hands keeping that woman out of the delivery room. Anna was still too busy mooning over Blade to be bothered with going out to a bar, and Heather couldn't blame her. That man was gorgeous.

That was fine, the four of them could have a dang good celebration by themselves.

"Woo hoo," she cheered as they clinked glasses and sipped their beverages.

"Don't look now, but I think that guy over there is eyeing you," Caitlin said to Heather.

She glanced at him. He was handsome, but he didn't have dark curly hair or green eyes.

"Damn, he's hot," Maya said.

"You're dating my brother," Heather said, frowning at her.

"What? I didn't say I wanted to hook up with him. Just that he's nice eye candy."

Shelby giggled and took another sip of her drink. "Mason would paddle my ass if I gawked at another man like that."

"All of our guys would," Maya said with a shrug. "Nothing wrong with keeping them on their toes."

"Speak for yourself. I don't have a man to answer to," Heather said.

"Ah, yes," Caitlin said, slapping her hand on the table. "No reason at all we drove all the way out to Little Rock to have some drinks."

"Nobody here believes that," Maya said, jumping in on Heather's ribbing. "Little Rock is miles and miles away from Big Roc."

"I need new friends," Heather muttered.

"What you need is to get laid," Caitlin added. "Telling you right now, it solves all kinds of problems."

"Eww, you're talking about my brother," Shelby said.

"Better get used to it right now," Heather said. "Maya holds nothing back about mine."

"Not true. I didn't tell you about the time he got ice cream and—"

Heather stuck her fingers in her ears. "La, la, la, la."

Everyone giggled.

"So what's the story with you and Roc?" Shelby asked. "I feel like there's something I'm missing."

"Nothing to tell."

"Ha!" Maya said. "He's got it bad for her, but for some reason, she won't give him the time of day."

"That's not it," Heather said softly.

"Oh, something did happen," Caitlin said, leaning in.

"He likes me—"

"A blind man can see that," Shelby said.

"But he won't act on it," she said slowly. "I'm not sure why. Don't know if it's how young I am. If it's his job, or my brother—"

"What? I can fix that," Maya said.

"No way. I don't want anybody twisting his arm."

Except her.

"Sweetie, sometimes men need a big smack in the face to make them see what they're missing," Maya said.

"And sometimes, Mr. Right Now can make things all better," Shelby said and nodded in the direction of the guy watching her. He lifted his glass in a wordless acknowledgement.

She turned back to the table. "I'm not using some guy to make Roc jealous. If it's the age thing, playing games will definitely make him think I'm some little girl."

"Nobody said anything about playing games," Caitlin said with a smirk. "But we see where your mind just went."

"Um, y'all don't need to knock games until you try them," Shelby said. She took another drink. Heather didn't think she was talking about the same kind of play, and no way was she going to ask.

"He's coming over," Maya whispered heatedly.

"*What?*"

She was going to kill all of her friends.

"Excuse me," he said in a voice so smooth controlled confidence exuded from it.

She turned around. "Yes."

Okay, he was ridiculously handsome up close. Dark hair and puppy dog brown eyes, tailored suit. He was probably around Roc's age, possibly a little older, but by the look in this man's eyes, he didn't care Heather was a good eight years younger than him.

"I know a man approaching a table full of women in a bar is cliché." He glanced around the table. "You all are very lovely." He looked at Heather then, his gaze unwavering. "But there's only one woman at this table I'd like to get to know."

Damn. That was good.

He didn't make her heart race or the blood rush in her veins, but she'd just met him. Maybe in time there'd be a spark ignited.

Like the one Roc had lit.

What had Shelby said about Mr. Right Now? Heather was young and beautiful. She was free to date anybody she wanted, and if Roc didn't want a chance with her, she needed to find a way to move on.

Or a way to smack him in the face.

She smiled at Mr. Right Now and stuck out her hand to shake his.

He lifted it to his mouth and kissed her knuckles.

"Heather Anderson," she said softly.

"Heather Anderson, the pleasure is all mine." He

released her hand right as a waiter came to the table with another round of drinks.

"We didn't order—"

"I did," the man said. "You ladies need to enjoy your night. This is my peace offering for intruding. Ms. Heather Anderson," he said with light inflection, reaching into his jacket and pulling out a couple of business cards and a pen. He handed her one. "Here's my number. May I have yours?" He put the other card face down so that the blank side was up and placed the pen on top of it. She smiled, took it, and jotted hers down.

"There you go."

"Now, I just need to think of the perfect date to ask you on."

"Don't wait too long,"

"Only a fool would do that." He winked "Ladies," he said, glancing at the others before turning and walking away.

"Wow, that was sorta hot," Shelby said.

"A man who sees what he wants and immediately goes after it. I wouldn't know how to act," Maya said.

"Right?" Caitlin asked, agreeing with her and taking a sip. "Going on a date all nice and normal like. Nobody getting shot at."

"Girl, don't even go there. My ass still hurts when I think of the first night Mason and I had together."

"He didn't even tell you his name," Caitlin said.

"It's probably hideous," Maya said. "Not that I'd know anything about that." She chuckled. Her boyfriend had the worst name in the history of names.

Heather turned the card over and read it. "Nope, it's completely normal."

"Luc with a C."

"Oh, like Roc with a C," Shelby said.

"He's about to get the shock of his life," Maya said.

"Shock? Maybe. Slap? Definitely," Heather said.

The girls at the table giggled and sipped their drinks, thoughts of Roc and boys in general dropped slipping further from their minds with every sip.

———

LUC STROLLED out of the bar and walked up to the stretch limousine parked out front. His driver stood holding the door open for him.

"Good evening, sir."

He nodded his appreciation for the respect he was due and got into the running limo. He opened his cell phone and hit the contact for his uncle.

"Ah, Luc, my boy. How's your trip?"

"Going well. I made contact. She doesn't recognize me."

"Excellent. And the other one?"

"Maya Carmichael didn't either. I'll proceed as planned."

"Good. Good. I don't need to remind you how important it is for this to work. The crime family in Dallas is crumbling. I can either take it by force or show I'm capable of exacting revenge. Making Maya suffer will make my job a lot easier.

"Is what she did that awful to the Oberman family? I know she was seeing Jake, but the guy was just muscle and a douche. Do you think anybody really gives a shit about him?"

"It's the sentiment. He's part of the family and was wronged. We're showing we put family first."

He'd told him this before, but he still didn't understand

why they didn't just force the other family's hand. This was the mafia, not T-ball. They didn't need approval from anyone to do a fucking thing.

"If this doesn't work, we'll kill the boss," his uncle said matter-of-factly.

That was more like it. "And if Heather realizes I was the one who kidnapped her?"

"Then we'll deal with her, too."

———

ROC IS COMING UP NEXT! In the meantime, check out ***Super Hot Supervisor***, the first in a fun, contemporary romance series!

———

HEY, y'all!

Thank you for reading my book. :) If you enjoyed it, I'd be very grateful for a review. If you didn't like it, then share that, too... as long as your review is honest, that's all that matters.

And ice cream. Ice cream matters, too.

Want the latest scoop? Be sure to sign up for my Newsletter! I mean, it's not as yummy as ice cream, but nothing ever is.

XOXO,
Mandy

ABOUT THE AUTHOR

Mandy Harbin is a *USA Today* Bestselling author who loves creating stories that explore the complexities of everyday relationships...with some kissing thrown in. She is a Superstar Award recipient, Reader's Crown and Passionate Plume finalist, and has achieved Night Owl Reviews Top Pick distinction many times. She also writes young adult romance as M.W. Muse because teens like kissing, too.

After graduating college and working many years in technology, she threw caution to the wind and began studying writing at the UALR. Years of trashed manuscripts and rejections eventually led to contracts and representation. With over thirty books published, she now serves on the board of her local writing chapter.

Mandy lives in a small, Arkansas town with her husband and their bossy dog, enjoying her own happily ever after...with some kissing thrown in.

mandyharbin.com/newsletter
facebook.com/Author.MandyHarbin
instagram.com/mandy_harbin
bookbub.com/authors/mandy-harbin

www.ingramcontent.com/pod-product-compliance
Lightning Source LLC
Chambersburg PA
CBHW050840190726
48286CB00007B/2161